LAST ONE HOME

LAST ONE HOME

Fred Stenson

NeWest Press

Edmonton

Copyright © 1988 Fred Stenson

All rights reserved. No part of this book may be reproduced in any form without written permission of the publisher.

First edition

Canadian Cataloguing in Publication Data

Stenson, Fred, 1951-
  Last one home

ISBN 0-920897-38-X (bound). — ISBN 0-920897-36-3 (pbk.)

1. Title.
PS8587.T46L3 1988   C813'.54   C88-091500-5
PR9199.3.S73L3 1988

Credits

Cover painting: Terry Bennett
Cover design: Bob Young/BOOKENDS DESIGNWORKS
Printing and binding: Hignell Printing Limited, Manitoba
Financial assistance:
    Alberta Culture
    The Alberta Foundation for the Literary Arts
    The Canada Council

Manufactured in Canada

NeWest Publishers Limited
Suite 204, 8631 - 109 Street
Edmonton, Alberta
Canada   T6G 1E8

For Susan

GABRIEL   Oh, give me a home

1

Gabriel was awake even before the phone call, and grappling with a dream he couldn't hold. Something about Jennifer, inside a room but a room white and horizonless like snow. Leona had tossed from her back to her side and the wave in the cheap waterbed had awakened him. She was having one of her nights and he stared at the black bread loaf shape of her, irrationally angry that she had disturbed his dream.

When he could not find the loose end of the dream, he tried to go back to sleep, but the feeling of being gypped out of something precious stayed with him and kept him awake. He liked dreaming about Jennifer and it didn't happen often anymore. She was a creature of the outdoors; he lived in classrooms and offices and apartment towers. His imagination had trouble bridging those things to make a dream.

Now that he was awake, he could not even think about her. Instead, men poured into his head, the kind he would have to face tomorrow in the job interview: serious men in suits. The men started asking questions and he started answering: iceberg-towing techniques, blowout-preventer disconnection steps. It was during this that the phone rang.

Leona jerked over, flopped an arm across his chest. "Come on, Gabriel. S'on your side."

He groped and found the receiver. A man's voice, familiar but not recognizable. The silence sent that message down the line and the voice said, "It's Joe."

Gabriel sat up then, swung his legs out of the bed so his ass balanced on the plank that kept the water mattress in. He dragged a hand down his face, slippery forehead, rasp of stubble. Still thinking of the interview, he imagined showering and shaving before he left. He also felt the outer edge of anger now that he knew who was keeping him from the sleep he needed.

"Can you hear me or what?"

"Ya, I hear you. What do you want?"

Throat clearing at the other end. Gabriel pulled the receiver back just in time to avoid the full impact of the hawk and spit.

"It's the Old Man."

Dead, Gabriel wondered.

"He's got a busted leg. They've got him in the hospital."

"Okay, that's news. But why phone me in the middle of the night?"

Joe spat again. "Thing is, I'm leaving down here."

"What do you mean, leaving?"

"The farm, I'm taking off." A radio station crept onto the line, bad country and western ricochet a hundred miles long. "I don't plan on being back."

"Joe, what the fuck are you saying? You want me to come run the place?"

"Whatever."

"Forget it. I just finished school. I've got job offers to follow up."

"Like I say, whatever. In case there's bad weather I gave the cows some feed this morning."

The line went dead.

Gabriel swiveled and fell back, the bed sloshing around him.

"Okay, you've got my attention. Who the hell was that?"

"My brother."

"Whoa. I didn't know you had one."

On Blackfoot Trail the next morning, in a coffee shop linked to a silent twelve-lane bowling alley. An acre of red arborite surrounded by wooden signs. Messages burned in the wood and varnished over. WASHROOMS THIS AWAY. NO CHECKS. Above the window into the kitchen, cute little signs with cute little sayings: "The hurrier I go the behinder I get."

Gabriel sat under a wagon wheel chandelier and sipped coffee. Beyond his egg-sticky plate, the morning tabloid lay open, his eyes pointing but not focussing there. It was only when the waitress came to pour more coffee that he realized he had been staring at today's Big Sky Woman. Eyebrow-length bangs cut straight across, face like a bruise. She had on a black halter top with fringes and, beneath that, a deep crease in her midriff as if the top of her body had been given a full turn. "Fame, eh?" Gabriel said as the waitress filled then overfilled his cup. She hurried away, tossing a bored 'yer welcome' back in the direction of his thanks.

There was a clock. Gabriel worked at not looking. He flipped the page and read about an ex-nun who had killed an Atlantic City realtor, her lover. She was enraged at him for taking her to a restaurant that served raw fish; shot him five times "right in the sushi bar." Right in the sushi bar: that would hurt.

He turned back to the cover story. A local stock analyst, unemployed, had held his postie at knife-point for seven hours demanding that trading in Devalta, a floundering development company, be stopped on all exchanges.

Gabriel pushed the paper aside. Looked everywhere the clock wasn't. For the first time, he heard what was coming out of the speaker above his head. British host of a local phone-in show, asking:

— But, madam, if it were your son?

— I wouldn't care.
— You wouldn't care!
— No, I wouldn't. If a son of mine raped and killed a little girl like this animal did, I'd say put him down like you would any mad dog.
— Your own flesh and blood.
— String him up and don't waste the taxpayer's money on him.

At a table to his right, six men Gabriel's age sat with elbows spread and baseball caps pointing to the centre of their huddle. The closest to Gabriel had the crack-of-ass-out-the-top-of-your-jeans look. An unlikely conversation about a foreman they all admired. Fined a guy fifty bucks for not getting his hair cut, then fired him a week later because the haircut he did get wasn't short enough. They all approved. "Rule's a fuckin' rule."

Then Gabriel did look at the clock and it was okay. The hour and minute of his interview was past. Two blocks away a roomful of men would be cursing his hide, drawing thick lines through his name on a short list. Asking what kind of nut-case, in an economy like this one, doesn't show up to be interviewed for a three thousand a month job?

Gabriel unlocked the door of his apartment. It bumped up against something cardboard, a box. Two other cardboard boxes were lined up behind it. Flaps closed, black felt pen inscriptions: BOOKS, KITCHEN, SUMMER CLOTHES. In the living room, a larger box stood open in the middle of the floor. With her back to him, Leona was unsucking the rubber cup of a toy basketball hoop from the wall. Oddly, she was singing the Stan Rogers lines

wanta see your smiling face
forty-five years from now.

She turned to throw the hoop into the box.
"Oh."
Gabriel tossed his jacket in the armchair, sat on top of it.
"Did I miss something?"
The hoop hit the box. Leona sat down too. She sat on the edge of the sheepskin-covered rocking-chair, he supposed so she would look poised to leave: someone who could not be coaxed to stay. Her long hands hung loose between the faded knees of her jeans.
"I thought I'd spare you the long explanations."
"Five months. I have to admit I'm curious."
She slid her hand onto the back of her neck, under the long lank hair. It looked a bit greasy. It was something he would remember: her endless search for a shampoo that lived up to its advertising. He was

already thinking of her as gone.

"Well, let me see. Your bed makes me seasick. You're on your way someplace for the summer. And, I might as well say it, our lovemaking hasn't exactly been shaming the gods lately. That's about it."

"Lousy lover too."

She lifted her face, with effort; smiled in a sad, sympathetic way. "Take it from someone who knows, good or bad isn't the issue; new or old matters more."

Four boxes, two suitcases, the rocking-chair, an armload of dresses on hangers in a dry-cleaner bag. A hug in the parking lot and gone. Gabriel had suggested a goodbye dinner but she'd already made plans.

The apartment, when he returned to it, had a plucked chicken look. The hissing and banging of the hot water heating seemed louder. He turned on the radio, cracked a beer and sat with it on the only remaining chair. The sky beyond the balcony had turned grey and was coming closer. A song ended and an excitable DJ said, "Time to put some wood on the fire and cuddle up on the bearskin, folks. The experts at the airport tell me there's a storm acomin'. She's gonna be cold, snowy and windy, not necessarily in that order. April in Alberta. In some places they call this spring."

A vision of cows bunched in the corner of a slab shelter, asses to the wind, icicles in their brisket hair ringing like chimes. They had feed yesterday but what about water? If it snowed enough they wouldn't leave shelter to find the dugout. If Joe had them at the feedlot, they'd be watering at the well but the tank might freeze.

He got up and went to the phone. Dialed from memory. Sheila Winterspeer answered and said that, yes, Walter *was* in. Not hard to tell that she thought he shouldn't be.

"Gabriel, is it really you?"

"How are you, Walter?"

"Good, good. You've heard about your father then."

"Joe called. Look, Walter, Joe's buggered off or something. He says the cows have feed for today but I don't know about water. Did it freeze hard overnight?"

"Well now, Gabriel, I'm not an absolute authority on today's weather. I can tell you that it *looks* grip-your-arse cold out there. Yes, Sheila confirms that storm warnings have been issued. I might add that this year shows signs of being the one without spring. The chinook has deserted us. The snow lies deep in the fields. Calves routinely shit themselves to death. The Great Spirit is not happy with His people."

"Do you happen to know if our cattle are watering at the dugout or the feedlot?"

"No, Gabriel, I do not. Would you like me to check?"
A pause of several seconds and, in that silence, a decision.
"No, that's alright. I'll be down."
"Good, then. I hope to see you."

Beyond the balcony, the first snow fell. Clouds so close to the ground they hung like gauze in the tops of trees. A few more hours and the snow would blow thick, drifts sifting up one another's backs. The cows locked by wind into the sheltered corner; tomorrow, licking up the last stems of hay from among the minarets of freezing shit. They would bawl into the wind expecting to draw a truck grill out of the grey. Calves among their legs taking the chill in deep.

Hank would love this, Gabriel thought. Told about it all, he would forget Joe's betrayal immediately. He would laugh out loud and insist on telling the guy trying to die in the bed next to him, "Five years gone but he's prodigal now, by Jesus. He's as good as down here."

Gabriel went to the bedroom, dragged his duffle bag down from the shelf above the hangers, threw it on the bed.

2

The storm turned the highway into a grey dead-end tunnel, poorly carved by Gabriel's headlights. At times when the snow shaped around a hill, the swirl would blind him. Drifts crept in from the highway's edge and, by Nanton, the truck had begun to whump into them, a sound that reminded Gabriel of being up north, of floatplanes taking off into whitecaps on Great Bear Lake. On all the Calgary radio stations, and then the Lethbridge ones as he passed into that parabola of sound, the DJ's were sternly warning. Don't drive unless you absolutely have to. Visibility down to forty yards in blowing snow. The RCMP were considering closure of Highway 1 east and west of Calgary, of Highway 2 south — along which his truck made its slow progress. Gabriel turned the radio off, leaving himself locked in a roar of engine and wind that was itself a kind of silence.

Staring into the vortex of snow, he fell hypnotized, a fog of mind that gave in to an impression of passing himself again and again going the other way. He could see that other self behind the wheel of the old half-ton, long ago traded away, whizzing up the summer highway north. He could even, at times, feel himself inside that five years younger man.

The picture was mostly funny: the velcro moustache and the loud plaid shirt he thought would look sharp and not out of place in the city, a departure from his usual embroidered cowboy ones. He sang most of the way. Songs like "Streets of Laredo" and "Ghost Riders in the Sky" that he only half-knew by heart.

But when the trance took him deeper, far enough inside the kid to actually feel, it was harder to laugh. The throat-swelling excitement, the sense that the old truck was covering more than miles, that it was a spaceship making a fiery exit from gravity's cling; he wouldn't have minded a little of that feeling now, in place of the dread.

Chewing down the long stretches of dull grey dark between the grain elevator towns, Gabriel devised a game to kill time. In the game, he was a university professor, a pedantic and slightly irritating one after the model of his friend Phipps. The other player was an earnest, ambitious type of student. The prof gives the student an assignment which is to write a paper listing the forces that propelled Gabriel up the highway to Calgary and university five years before. It isn't a research paper; the student can have for the asking all the facts he needs.

In possession of the topmost layer of information, the student jumps to a predictable conclusion: that Gabriel's job at a gas plant near Beaver Creek and his troubled romance with Jennifer, the schoolteacher, were between them enough to move him on. Gabriel's bosses at the plant had lifted him out of the ranks of the wrench and paintbrush boys, to study for a fourth class steam ticket on company time, the paper he would need to be an operator. They often suggested he had what it took to go still further, to university and a degree in engineering. As well, Gabriel and Jennifer were bickering in the basement suite they shared.

The professor arches an eyebrow. He pops the top of his ballpoint in and out against his teeth. Are you sure you're not mistaking cause for effect, he asks? How do you explain that, two years before, Gabriel had been sitting in a tavern with his two best friends, Dalton Pressley and Jimmy McCrimmon, and that the three had piled their hands in the wet centre of the table and sworn an oath? Drunkenly but solemnly, they swore that none of them would ever leave Beaver Creek. If you think Gabriel was just drunk or had his fingers crossed, you're wrong; he'd never meant anything as much in his life.

All three of them were disgusted with the pricks who were leaving Beaver Creek almost daily to go to school in the city or to chase some big buck job up north. The three had decided proudly to stay behind and make it hard for any of the other kind who tried to slip back in.

No, to truly explain Gabriel's departure, the student must find the reasons why this oath was broken.

So the student goes off and comes back with Gabriel's family life in hand. The trio of men on the farm locked for years in some competitive, mostly silent state of bitterness. Hank, the Old Man, making life as hard for his sons as he could. Working them like slaves, making fun of them even as they did his work for him. What better motivation for departure could there be than that?

Better, the professor admits, closer. But it had been like that since Gabriel was a kid. Hank had always been mean and pestering. And yet, Gabriel made no move to leave until he was almost nineteen years old. In fact, if you look and listen closely to the scene of Hank and Gabriel atop the hill west of the farmhouse in the fall of that year, you'll see that Hank is *telling* Gabriel to go. Saying, "Damned if I'll have any lazy Indian sonofabitch laying around my farm not earning his keep."

Put in the student's shoes at this point, Gabriel admits he would probably give up.

Gabriel reached and fingered the cords in the back of his neck. They'd started to cinch up as they always did on the highway. He pushed his fingers into the muscle on the right side so it shot out a sliver of pain. Faint reminder of the fiercer hurt that used to be there and was such an essential clue to the mystery he would have the student solve.

The professor addresses the student:

See here: the part of the story where Dalton, Jimmy and Gabriel are getting together every Sunday at Gabriel's or Dalton's farm. See how they run in a spoiled two-year-old or a cantankerous old gelding — or, failing that, a cow to buck for them.

In particular, look at a Sunday in late July, when the three of them are at Dalton's place and Dalton's old man has said no to using more of his stock for their damn rodeo. Two Sundays before, they'd spooked a young filly so bad that, when Dalton's father tried to catch her, she'd leapt out a pole corral and didn't stop until she was through two fences and into a neighbour's wheat.

So they sat under a tree, the three of them, and drank what was left of Saturday's beer, watched grasshoppers flick between brittle stems of grass. They got bored and more bored until Jimmy said, Hey! and outlined a contest he'd imagined.

Out on the cracked hardpan of a cattle working pen, behind a slab fence so they couldn't be seen, Dalton and Gabriel sat their horses at opposite ends with Jimmy calling instructions in the middle. He held a flag he'd fashioned out of a snow fence picket and a snot rag.

"It's called a joust," he'd told them, "like knights used to do with spears." He dropped the flag and Dalton and Gabriel rode at one another, spinning their ropes and then throwing for each other's heads. Dalton threw too soon and almost snared the front legs of Gabriel's horse. Gabriel let fly about right but, having thrown his, Dalton had time to lie flat along his pinto's neck so the rope skimmed over him and off the heel of his saddle.

They went at it all day like that, taking turns, until at last Dalton caught Jimmy. There'd been a lot of talk about what would happen but what did occur took them by surprise. Caught round the chest, Jimmy ripped out of the saddle so fast the motion was barely visible. His feet came straight out of the overly large pair of boots Dalton had lent him and, if they hadn't, he would have broken one or both legs. He hit the grey trampled ground so hard he bounced and a lot of skin tore off his hips and elbows before Dalton could pull his horse up. It seemed amazing that Jimmy was able to yank the rope off himself and run around limping and cursing.

If it had stopped there, then maybe Gabriel wouldn't be passing himself today. Or, at least, the escape would have found some other cause. But they didn't stop, even though the game was guaranteed to maim the next one to lose; that was what made Gabriel's mind up in the end.

There were five Sundays in August that year and, by the fifth, no one was joking or talking. Each rider was too deep in his strategy and in his fear. Jimmy was sullen and almost resigned; he'd been the only one caught and he knew that was not just accident. Jimmy was a town kid and less skillful with rope and horse. What had been saving him was that Dalton and Gabriel wanted each other more.

Jimmy dropped the flag. The horses drove off their hind legs and, grunting, poured themselves forward. Dalton wove a huge figure eight above his head. Gabriel spun a much smaller loop. Gabriel's plan was to throw first, come in under. He saw his small tight loop go straight for its destination, the front edge hitting Dalton above the eyebrows, below the hat. Dalton threw in a panicky way in that instant. The back edge of Gabriel's loop came in higher than the front; it flicked away Dalton's hat but did not snare him. Dalton's big loop came and Gabriel thought to catch the lazy thing and fling it aside. His hand closed on air.

The rope dropped round him. Gabriel tore at it, getting it as far as his neck before the lariat sizzled through the hondo and ripped into him. The rope ate into his neck and between the ribs on the other side, uprooting him fiercely. The ground slugged him. The rope slacked for an instant as Dalton's horse hesitated, then flashed and bit as the horse spooked forward. That was the motion that whipped his neck and sent a pain like a hot wire out of his shoulders and into his brain.

He remembered nothing more until Dalton and Jimmy were pulling the rope off him. Laughing in a crazy way, Dalton put a boot on Gabriel's chest and beat his own with a beller of victory.

The student frowns, doesn't get it exactly when the professor says that this is it, the exact moment that sliced off the past and made way for the present. Can't you see, says the professor, how Dalton and Jimmy were left standing on the hardpan, and how, when they dropped in to see Gabriel a few times afterward, they always found him cool, as if he didn't want to know them anymore? And the good rig job Gabriel had? He never went back to it. When he took to sitting around at home, doing nothing every day but climb the hill west of the farmhouse, not even helping with the harvest, it drove his father to climb the hill and tell him to go. "You lazy half-Indian sonofabitch . . ." Which is how he came to take a labouring job at the gas plant, and how he came to meet up again with his old schoolteacher, Jennifer; both events leading in their way to his eventual departure for university.

All explained. But, as the professor and the student in Gabriel unite again, he's not sure. It *is* the order in which things happened; and it *did* begin when his neck whipped and his mind was drenched in pain . . .

The windshield wipers batter back and forth, balled with frozen slush. The dizzy swirl of snow beyond is like the juggle of balls in a TV bingo basket. For the sake of the student, he could say something folksy like, "If you want to teach a pig not to cross a fence, the surest way is to put a hundred volts through the barbwire." But it wasn't so much the pain his family and his friends had already caused him that did it; it was the greater pain they were destined, even doomed to cause each other if he stuck around.

Gabriel pulled over onto what he hoped was the shoulder of the road. He rolled the window down and squeezed his body out to thumb ice from the wiper blades.

3

On that August day five years ago, the trip from Beaver Creek to Calgary had taken two hours. Today's journey back seemed endless. Hugging the tail-lights of a car in front, Gabriel hit the ditch south of Claresholm and spent an hour digging his truck and his pilot car back onto blacktop. At the Fort Macleod turning, he tucked in behind a snowplow and let it lead him the rest of the way west. When he left it for the gravel road, north again, it was both storm-dark and night.

The drifts were more substantial and taller on the gravel road, wider and tougher. When he burst through them, showers of snow shot over the hood and roof. In each drift, there was an uncertain second, the truck dragging, then a surge forward and relief.

Then, on a curve, his headlights picked up a drift like a house and no way round it. The first instinct was to gun the engine but, as it loomed to a height twice the truck's, Gabriel slammed his brakes. The truck sideslid to a halt against its flank.

Gabriel turned off the engine. Considering he was still in the middle of a storm, it was quiet. From behind the seat he dragged a parka that unleashed an old smell of grain dust, gasoline and sweat as it unfolded. Stepping out, Gabriel understood the reason for the quiet. He was in a lee behind the snowbank with the wind whinnying far above. He left his duffle bag in the locked cab and began to flounder up the drift's soft side.

The walk brought to mind a saying common to old farts everywhere: that it has to warm up to snow. As long as he kept the top of his hood pointed into the north wind he was comfortable. In a darkness unnervingly total, he kicked through invisible puffs of substance, staggered through stiffer banks. Falls into soft depth informed him that his steps had curved out of plumb with the road.

Starting out, he'd been afraid he would pass the turn but, as he walked, the snow lost some of its fury and he could see dim aureoles of farm light. Opposite the first glimmer he groped until he found the mailbox. He struck a match between his body and its metal hood. In the brief light he read "Carlson," which left Ziegler, Christoff and Winterspeer before he was home. He had only begun.

Four miles and who knew how much time later, he came to Winterspeer's turning. For a second it seemed the best possible thing was to take that turn and follow it down to his friend. Winterspeer would fill a glass with whisky. Make him laugh. Invite him to stay. Another feeling swept that one aside. A desire to be in the farmhouse. To stand alone among the ghosts, friendly and unfriendly.

He began to count his steps. A precise half-mile stood between Winterspeer's gate and Hank's. A kind of dread excitement mounted as he found his own road and turned in, the wind hitting him now from the side. The slender road with its centre hump of gravel traced along the curve of the hill. He found it easier to stay in this dished-out track but his sense of where he was fooled him. More than once he falsely felt the change from rise to fall that marked the final drop into the farmyard, and he felt nothing when he did actually reach and pass that point. Only when he walked into a post that had always marked a washout on the side of the road did he know for certain he was moving downhill.

Once he passed that certain landmark, Gabriel knew exactly where he was and what he was not seeing. On the right, the shoulder of the hill concealed the farmhouse from the main road. On that hill was also the place where his grandfather Baptiste was buried, standing up: the family's only major legend. To the left, west, he was not seeing the hill he liked to think of as his own. It was the hill he'd most liked to climb as a kid, also the one he'd made his father climb the day Hank kicked him out. Beyond that was an even stronger presence unseen: the Livingstone Range of the Rocky Mountains; a silver wall and, if you knew where to look, The Gap, a narrow slot by which the Old Man River left the Rockies for the foothills and prairie, and through which the elk herds streamed when the snows forced them out in search of grass and farmer's hay.

Below where he walked, Gabriel was not seeing the unpainted outbuildings of the farm, clustered around the house. At one time there had been a yardlight but Gabriel supposed the bulb had burned out and never been replaced.

The next thing he felt with certainty was the change of pitch as the road beneath him spilled and fanned into the flat. If he stared hard enough, the indefinite shapes of barn and house seemed to suggest themselves. But he was possibly just imagining a difference in the black. Then he fell.

Reaching back, he released the barbs from his pantlegs and bootlaces. Typical. It wouldn't be the Old Man's place if you couldn't trip on your face over a tangle of wire or bust a shin on a grass-rooted piece of machinery.

More cautious now when he stood up, he felt the air, kicked out with his feet, finding in this way the box of the grain truck, the door panel, the bulging fender, the blind socket of a missing headlight. Three confident strides farther and he stood in the gate, two simple pine posts which had always been called "the gate" though a fence had never joined them. For that matter, no gate had ever hung between.

Hand on the screen door latch, the feeling of dread mixed with excitement took him again. He pulled the screen back and reached for the knob on the door inside. The space between doors had sifted full of snow which he pawed away with his glove. Then, the still of indoors, the cement floored porch, the smell of sour milk creeping up his nostrils like a living thing. It sharpened his sense of where he was, in what kind of place. Here, milk and cream were split on a hand-cranked separator. Raw milk spilled and was never cleaned up except by the tongues of cats. Left to rot and reek and feed into the larger pool of smells: outhouse, barn, chicken coop, yard. The mingled stench of shit and decay. At school in town, his teachers had taught that smell was a source of pleasure. But at home the stinks far outnumbered the aromas.

He groped for the string in the centre of the room. Found it, pulled it — nothing happened. When he reached around to the switch inside the kitchen and got the same result, he realized that more was at work here than carelessness. The power was off, the line from the main road to the farm whipped off by wind.

I am in the dark, he told himself and laughed. Wasn't that the truth?

Gabriel stepped up across the second threshold, through the doorless doorway into the kitchen. The brittle linoleum crackled under his boots and he was struck by the fact that, even at the beginning of this day, he would have taken off his boots before entering any house. Even if the host had told him to keep them on, he would have felt guilty. Here, he walked in, returning automatically to a lack of rule that had spread silently through the place sometime after his mother died. Three men, without women, living like pigs.

Across the kitchen he found the storage closet door, behind which he was fairly sure a lamp or flashlight could be found. Then he closed it without even feeling inside; his answer to an impulse almost sexual that said, explore without light. He would find out how much was left of the sense that had once let him whisper down the stairs and through the rooms, arriving for a piss off the front step without barking a shin on anything.

The arborite table was touched, the divide between kitchen and living room crossed. He felt with his boot toe the edge of the hooked rug. The strong smell of cigarette smoke that had taken over from milk reek in the kitchen was different here, smoke still but of a different kind. He wondered if what he smelled could possibly be the scent of pipe left in the wallpaper and furniture by his grandfather Baptiste. Gabriel blew out and drew in deeper hoping to savour that childhood smell, but somehow he breathed beyond that stratum and found another, which he could have sworn was woman's perfume. Except that he couldn't remember his mother having any scent but her own, he could have fancied he was breathing her back within these walls.

Two steps inside the living room and he stopped, just as he might have done seven or a dozen years before. His father, brother and he had done their sitting in the kitchen, the living room being too comfortable for the tense brand of conversation they specialized in. For the Old Man's diatribes and for Joe's constipated talk, the kitchen was a better place; closer to the door and escape.

Gabriel retreated. Backed out of that tomb of his mother, the main enticement drawing him to this house. Her piano would be there, her pictures, her flower design doilies; the latter no doubt yellowed and crusted with dust and neglect. He might try later, approaching with more careful thoughts.

Finding the first step of the open stairway, Gabriel began to climb. The extra sense failed him here for his toes struck the back panel of each step. The years away had taught him deeper steps, less steep. More familiar was the smell, stronger as he went. The stink of Joe's feet. Like a dead sheep tied to each ankle was what he used to say across the shared upstairs whenever Joe undressed them.

At the top of the stairs, Gabriel stopped again. He didn't want to be here either. In the entire upstairs, there was not a single finished wall, just the raw two-by-four frame that divided it into crude reservations. He imagined that his own mattress would be where it had been but would be piled under with junk — stinking junk like hoof trimmers and bloodied calf pullers — just a little something to let him know, if he ever did come back, how little he'd been missed. No amount of child's remote control could find a path through this. He retreated down the stairs.

The desire to snoop had spent itself and he thought he would find a lamp and covers, and sleep on the couch. But, as he reached the arch into the living room, the feeling came back with a rush; a real lust this time, to cross the living room and enter the one place in the house always off-limits. His heart actually beat faster as he made the few steps between the couch and the piano bench to the door of his father's bedroom.

The hinges squawled. Inside, he took another deep breath to analyze. Again, a surprise. Expecting saddle soap, a too-strong brand of men's cologne, or leather, his nostrils filled with a much stronger whiff of perfume. No sooner had he marked this than a woman's voice, shaking but strong, barked out of the black.

"There's a gun pointing at you, buster. It's a shotgun so I'm not apt to miss. Move a muscle before I hear you talk and you're dead."

"Who the hell are you?"

"I'd say that's my question."

"My name's Gabriel. . . . I used to live here."

It didn't sound like enough reason for her not to shoot him.

A rustle of sheets. A deep breath blown out. There was a lot of other commotion and, finally, a match plumed. Gabriel saw that, son of the house or not, he was still staring across the curlicue bedstead into the tunnel of a twelve gauge shotgun. The barrel was balanced on her feet, the stock and trigger loop held awkwardly in one hand as the other hand held the match.

"Jesus, Jesus," the woman behind it muttered. The feet fell apart and the gun barrel dropped onto the quilt. The match reached her fingers; she cursed and threw it away. She lit another and held it to the wick of a kerosene lamp on the night table, setting the glass back around the fire. She looked up and Gabriel shifted his gaze to the dresser and mirror.

"I'll tell you kid, you almost wound up splattered on the wall. I said to myself, I ain't moving. Let the bugger come to me and he'll be damn sorry. . . "

"You always sleep with a shotgun?"

"I'm not used to being alone at night."

Gabriel stared at the off-kilter blond hair, the make-up smeared in sleep. Her age he couldn't guess, anywhere between forty and fifty-five. Hank's woman, he thought, and slid into an easy dislike. There was still some mystery, though; Hank didn't as a rule let them stay.

"Well," she said. A long-fingered hand extended. "Pleased to meet you, I think. Lyla Pryde."

He took her hand, felt the strength of the handshake, the muscles of the arm knotting up behind the grip.

"You aren't exactly a frequent visitor," she went on. "Pardon me for asking what the hell you're doing here tonight."

"Joe phoned. Said the Old Man was in hospital and that he was clearing out. He didn't mention you."

"No, I suppose he wouldn't. And you came galloping to the rescue."

"I don't like cows dropping dead, which is what I imagine Hank would've let happen, being too cheap to hire anybody."

Lyla had been leaning forward, now she leaned back. She drew up the sheet and regarded him with disappointment. "He speaks highly of you."

Gabriel laughed unpleasantly. "I bet he does."

"Well, if all you want to do is run down your father, you can get out of his bedroom. Take the lamp. I don't need it."

By lamplight, Gabriel reclimbed the stairs. He found Joe's mattress in the mess and, even in the low light, could see that the scrawl of sheets hadn't been washed in recent memory. He squared them and climbed aboard, staying dressed for protection. He wrapped the pillow in his parka before putting his head there. He tried to think of his mother, then, to enjoy a portion of what he'd imagined as he approached down the road. A solitary night with her, her house, her memory, her things scattered around. But now, when he tried, he could only draw together the tired shards of recollection that always came to mind. Hank had done it again. Lying in bed two dozen miles away, he'd set a trap and, ever obedient, Gabriel had fallen in.

He raised the carboned glass and blew away the soft plume of fire. If there were such things as ghosts, he thought, his mother's must have a better place to be than here.

4

Gabriel woke up embarrassed. He'd been in his father's bed with Lyla. She had his head in a choking armlock of passion and he was just about to thrust. He was thankful the real Lyla chose that moment to drop a frying pan.

The parka had shifted and Gabriel was clutching Joe's greasy pillow to his face. He threw it aside. Looking around, he couldn't see far for the piles of gear on all sides. In the light it was even grottier than he remembered. On a wooden box beside the mattress stood a lamp, a painted rose on a green stem visible among scratches on the base. A waxy paper shade, bunged in on one side. The box was left over from the days when Japanese oranges came in wood, a crispy label with a faded orange clung to one side. On the nearest two-by-four Joe had hung a tin mirror by a nail.

Walling this bedroom were successively larger hills of things owned by Joe. The closest contained his barbells, a snowmobile suit, wool socks in stinking balls, a suit of long underwear with a stain down the crotch ("brown stars" they'd called them as kids). The goods of fall formed the top of the hill behind that, with summer's dirty laundry holding it up. Gabriel stood up out of the mess and looked around for something of his. He recalled leaving his duffle bag in the truck and that brought the news that he couldn't even shave. The racket of a pan rubbing back and forth downstairs rooted him to the spot. He didn't want small talk or an offer of breakfast. He didn't want food that meant more than food.

Crossing by the kitchen on his way to the bathroom, Gabriel muttered good morning but did not look. Some sound came back from her as he was closing and locking the door. What he saw when he turned shocked him. New tub, new toilet, new sink. Above the tub were actual tiles with a shower head sticking out of them. Linoleum, a little shag rug on the floor. What's more, these things looked clean.

Nothing could have struck Gabriel as more revolutionary in the house of his father. Hank made it a point of pride never to spend money on the trivial acts of washing and emptying. Joe and Gabriel had been the ones to build a bathroom here in the first place, a rare act of cooperation in rebellion against the long walk to the outhouse. While they installed the toilet and tub, Hank had leaned in the doorway making fun of them. What kind of pansies had he raised here? Were they going to put in a mirror too so they could put on eye shadow and curl their hair? And where was the water going to come from? What were they going to do for ideas when they flushed the last gallon of drinking water down their fancy shitter?

It had to be the woman, Lyla.

Gabriel washed his face and grabbed a toothbrush off a rack of them. The towel he dried off with was fresh and smelled of her. He stepped out of the can with a refusal of breakfast on his lips but the kitchen was empty. She'd set up a Coleman stove across the powerless burners and, atop it, a pot of coffee simmered. A frying pan lay upside down on the counter, drying. He looked out the window but could see no sign of her. He couldn't see much of anything for the storm was on again and the view of the buildings choked by snow.

In Joe's snowmobile suit with his own parka overtop, Gabriel pushed out the door. The snow was all round the house in high tapering dunes. Tails of new snow whispered round the peaks, building them steadily higher. This was the blizzard the old farts would measure by for a decade. "The spring of '85, by God now, that was some blizzard!"

Gabriel beat his way over to the Old Man's four-by-four. He pawed down a drift and tried the driver's door. It was cow-kicked in the middle and the hinges gave a terrific yowl. The smell of Hank was inside, hair oil mainly and ashtray. The engine growled in a surly way but caught. He went around to the rear and kicked a vent for the exhaust, found a shovel in the back and dug, ten feet back and ten feet forward. Then he tried it. He blasted out of the first drift, scrunched to a halt in the second. He double-checked that he'd been in four-wheel drive and, when he saw that he had been, he gave up.

He picked a hayhook off the cab floor and was feeling in the box for an axe when Lyla ducked out of the barn aboard a horse he didn't recognize. She had her cowboy hat tied on with a wool scarf that covered her ears. Two wood-handled hayhooks jangled on her saddle. The big black plunged its chest through a drift, promptly fought the bit and tried to turn back. Good luck, thought Gabriel.

He watched her just long enough to size up the direction she was trying to go. Certain then where the cattle must be, he took his hayhook and axe to the fenceline. Sinking his mitt into the snow, taking hold of the top wire and letting it slide through his grip, he drove his thighs into the crusted drifts. He progressed slowly down the valley.

A long hour later, Gabriel reached the feedlot. He had to fight to lift his legs from plank to plank over the fence and, at the top, he let himself fall over into the pillow of snow. From the top of the fence he had been able to see the red-brown cattle mobbed in the corner of the slab windbreak. For the moment, he was too beat to work his way over to them. He dug an alcove next to the slabs and sat massaging his thighs. If the Old Man were here, he would have drawn on some perverse strand of steel to remain standing. He would have rolled a smoke and said, thought you were in shape.

Getting up, Gabriel squinted at the one hope he had of feeding the cows today. The corner where the cattle crushed was the outside of the unused feedlot. For ten years, Hank had been selling his calves in the fall. Before that, he had wintered them here. Back then, Joe and Gabriel had built a lean-to roof over the feedlot bed ground. They'd hauled round bales up on top, placed them two-deep across the poles and wire. The bales would be rotten and musty by now, if they were there at all, but they were also the only hope of feed.

When the cattle saw Gabriel wading the snow toward them, they milled to face him, bawling. A human of any kind meant food. Their ice-encrusted faces and the pink-ribbed roofs of their hollering mouths were all around him as he entered the warmth of their bed ground. Frantic as they were, the cows weren't in particularly tough shape. Probably hadn't digested or even chewed all of what was in their four stomachs.

The calves were another matter. The odd one was up bunting its mother's udder but most lay curled in a line along the foot of the slab fence. Here and there, Gabriel could see one in trouble. A small roan, late-born, had chilled so deep its shivers were staggers. Pushing past the cows he found another, standing stupidly exposed to the wind. Ahead of its hipbones, the sides were caved in together; the eyes were sunk into the skull. It was so inert it made no move to run as Gabriel swapped it end for end to see the wet smear of yellow down its ass. This, he hadn't thought of, that the calves might be scouring. He imagined the plastic bottle in the porch cupboard, the black crusted spoon held to it by an elastic band. His forgetting to bring the powder probably meant the end for this calf and perhaps others.

In the shelter's corner, Gabriel began to climb. At the top of the slabs his knee struck a prickle of hay under the snow. Up here the blowing snow stung like sand. He stood in the full blast of it, stabbed his hook through the white and brought up black: a core of rotten hay. A cloud of dust came too. He breathed only a bit as the wind took it fast away but it made him cough. This was a problem for another day and he threw the light shards down, bouncing them off the crowded backs. Tongues reached and wrapped in the black shit, even before it hit the ground. Candy to them.

When half the roof's covering was off and down, Gabriel climbed inside the feedlot and found the straw. Mice had eaten the twine and mice of all ages fell out as he picked up armloads to haul across to the cows. He packed it in and around the calves, a losing battle in that the cows were eating the cover off their offspring between one trip and the next.

Then Gabriel had to rest again. He slumped down between sleeping calves against the fence. He was weakly fighting sleep when Lyla Pryde muscled up through the snow, the wind at her back. She walked to where he was sitting, looked around the cattle who were mostly sneezing and coughing by now.

"That black crap will make them cough for a month."

Gabriel stayed where he was, leaned back, felt the bark side of the slab through his coat. His one arm rested across a shivering calf. In her sheepskin coat, the lining rolled out into a warm noose, Lyla looked fit and capable, aggressively so.

"Any better ideas?"

"There's a stack of good hay up there about half a mile." She pointed north.

"Good. I'll wait here."

"I could haul it down behind Gallant."

"Gallant is your horse?"

She nodded.

"Too bad. If he was a Nodwell all-terrain vehicle, you might have a chance. Being a horse, if you rest him good and lead him home, he may not die of pneumonia."

She shifted her stance, locked in the other hip; looked away and bunged her hayhook into the palm of her glove.

"What's your plan, then, genius?"

Gabriel pointed at the cows, still eating between coughs. "They're fed already. Next thing is to get some water out of the pump down there. Beat a trail. They'll be thirsty when they finish."

"I'll help you make trail — if I'm permitted."

"Free country."

Gabriel stood up.

"You've got a plaster of yellow calf shit on your leg," Lyla told him.

"Good. It'll remind me that half of these calves are scoured."

"The scour powder's in my saddlebag. We can dope calves after they've watered."

Gabriel started for the pump house, Lyla behind him and a chain of bawling cows bunched behind her. At some point, Lyla passed him and broke trail the rest of the way. The trough was empty. The cattle mobbed it anyway, the ones in back threatening to knock the ones in front over the rim.

"Do you know when this pump was used last?" Gabriel asked.

"Not since I've been here."

"I don't know how long that is."

"Ten months."

He drove the shed door open with a shoulder, climbed in. An ancient pump engine stood there on a plank platform, a huge cast-iron affair that belonged in a museum. Gabriel pulled pieces of rag out of a can of oil and, without much hope, poured it on everything that was expected to move. Then he flung the flywheel until his arms were leaden, without producing a single kick. He began to undo the assembly that geared the engine into the trunk of the pump. He found the wooden pump handle and wired it into place. He realized he was too tired in the arms to do any more. Lyla stood inside the shed door, waiting.

"Okay," said Gabriel, "I'm tired and if you help me we may get some water to these cows today."

She brushed by him, took the handle and swung it with vigour.

Back at the bed ground, Gabriel asked for the scour powder. Lyla went back for it and Gabriel made a list in his head of the calves most in need of doping. When Lyla came back she was on her horse, feeding out a loop through the hondo of her lariat.

"That one looks the worst," she said, pointing.

Gabriel grinned inwardly; he had the flaw he'd been looking for.

"Look, Annie Oakley, the last thing these cows need right now is you tearing around in the middle of them playing rodeo. Does this calf look like it needs roping?" He reached and caught the roan by its weak kicking back leg. "Just give me the powder."

Lyla jerked up her rope, coiled it and slapped it on the saddle horn. She reached in under the flap of the saddlebag, tossed the powder bottle and spoon on the ground. The gelding wheeled and galloped through the gap in the bank of snow. Catching calves, flipping them, kneeling on them while he spooned powder between their stiff jaws, Gabriel felt good. A second wind had restored him.

5

Deep inside his rubber overboots, moccasin liners and wool socks, Gabriel could feel a general hurt and a few high notes that were probably blisters, friction chafing out spots of pain on his winter-soft skin. Otherwise, he felt good, muscle-sore but refreshed from the sleep he'd had.

When he'd arrived back at the farm from the feedlot, his legs had been stone, his thoughts ricocheting like bullets in a barrel. He was starving and had thoughts of taking a chicken out of the coop, wringing its neck and roasting it feathers and all. Instead he found a chocolate bar in his truck catch-all. After eating that, he'd climbed the ladder into the barn loft and slept for two hours burrowed in the straw.

Now, walking into Winterspeer's yard, he felt silly going so far to avoid Lyla. She wasn't a dragon; he could probably explain himself and end the war. But even as he thought these things, he wasn't sure he'd try to make it any different.

Sheila opened the door for him and said simply, "Gabriel." A kid stood behind her, an eight or nine year old, and it took some seconds to figure out that this was not a visitor but Tom, their son.

"Walter's in the living room. Come."

Gabriel kicked off his boots, dumped his parka, pushed away the dog as it tried to sniff him in the crotch. Walter met him under the arch into the living room and pumped his hand heartily.

"Two day's beard and all," he said and led him by the elbow into the larger room. "Sit down. I have saved a bottle for exactly this occasion."

Sheila came in too, stayed long enough to have a small gin. She led the small talk, asked him about his trip through the storm, about university, his city life. She avoided all mention of the reason for his return. Then, as she customarily did, Sheila got up and left the room, knowing it would free up their conversation and not wanting to hear that freer conversation anyway. She looked good, thought Gabriel, watching her go. Hadn't aged and probably wouldn't for a long time still; she had that quality. But Winterspeer was grizzled. The full round cheeks had also withdrawn into crevices sometime in the last five years. Deeper creases framed the pale blue eyes.

"I know," said Walter, catching him. "Winterspeer is no longer young. They say smoking causes wrinkles, as does the parching sun, the filthy drying wind. We have no chance here. We wither and become in the end a damn poor harvest."

"You don't look so bad."

"Thanks for the polite lie. Here, give me your glass. I'll fetch ice."

In the minute that Winterspeer was out of the room, Gabriel sensed eyes on him and turned to find Tom peering round the door-frame. Gabriel started to ask him how he was but the boy jumped back out of sight. Then Winterspeer was back with the bottle and a tray of ice.

"Stupid kid," he said. "A day off school and he's bushed. He's growing up to be a farmer, you know. Grand irony. I dreamt for him an escape into high society and what does he do but follow in his mother's and maternal grandparents' footsteps. Down that long furrow that eventually you cannot climb out of with ropes. Asks to drive the tractor. Displays that sure sign of a hard life: mechanical aptitude." Winterspeer took a slurp from his glass, squinted hard at Gabriel. "But then, being mechanical hasn't damned you to a hard life, or has it?"

"Up until today, I thought I was headed for a pretty easy one."

"Bastard of a storm! My true fate came upon me today. At my own instigation, Sheila fitted me with harness and I dragged bales through neck deep snow. To cows which, I will say right now, were deeply unappreciative. You're not going to stay, are you?"

"As soon as Hank gets back on his feet, I'm out of here. He and his Amazon can have it back anytime."

Winterspeer frowned, drank, lit a cigarette off the live end of the last one. Gabriel reached and took one from Walter's pack and smoked too.

"You've met Lyla then," Walter said. "I didn't know if she was there or staying in town."

"She's there alright. Almost shot me last night. Had a shotgun in bed with her."

"Then you're lucky to be alive. I would say Lyla could finish what she starts."

"I wouldn't know. We're not on speaking terms."

"Difference of opinion about your father, I suppose."

Gabriel laughed at the understatement and Winterspeer carried on.

"I don't want to seem to be siding against you, but the woman impresses me. She has character."

"What the hell's going on over there, Walter? Since when does my old man allow females under his roof for more than a few hours at a time?"

"I think Lyla has worked considerable changes in Hank."

"You're not going to tell me that he's a great guy all of a sudden."

"From my vantage, Hank remains what he's always been. What that is I refuse to say. He sometimes drops by to comment on the former golden age of this farm, before I came along, or to tell me that a few of my cows are eating his grass and he won't stand for it."

Gabriel watched Winterspeer's eyes as he spoke. The Scotch bottle had not been "saved" in any virgin sense. The eyes already contained the bloodshot passion Winterspeer could usually find in a bottle.

"As for my opinion of Hank, I refuse to say a word. You'll scoff at this, but there is an absolutely tenacious tendency for fathers and sons, sooner or later, to reconcile." Gabriel grunted. "I know, I know, but it is my rule of thumb and I'm sticking to it. Besides, you know my opinions about your father, in that you are the source of most of them."

Winterspeer went to the fire and kicked a piece of cedar fencepost deeper into the flames. "I will tell you this much, though: people of this community have been wont to compare me to your father and it is not a comparison I particularly relish."

Gabriel made another face.

"No, no," Winterspeer continued, "it's true. Our neighbours, as you know, intellectualize mainly by comparison. To define you, they compare you to the familiar. I was not familiar and so caused them difficulty, but they persevered and finally settled on the idea that I was like Hank."

"Hand me the bottle. I need to wash that one down."

"I do not care for the comparison but I do understand it. We smoke, we drink, we work less than the accepted community standard. But, most importantly in the eyes of the people roundabout, we were both womanizers. This was crucial and this was the aspect against which I rebelled. Not because Hank actually did sleep with a stable of women whereas my admiration was bestowed chastely from afar, but because your father's mentality toward women is abhorrent to me."

Winterspeer stood, waved his glass, sent an amber wave close to the rim.

"I, as poet, see Woman as muse. I deeply admire Woman — even when women in the more earthly sense are kicking the living shit out of me. I love Woman and have done since my earliest day of nipple worship. I love Her still. Your father, on the other hand.... I say no more." Winterspeer thumped down in his chair.

"Amen, anyway," said Gabriel, raising his glass in salute.

"But!" shouted Winterspeer, slamming his own now empty glass to the table and bringing Sheila's head around the corner for an indignant instant, "but something has changed. In Lyla, your father has admitted a woman under his roof and into his life. I have seen them riding together. A striking silhouette against the evening sky. I think, though I don't know, that your father has changed."

"I can't believe it," Gabriel said.

"I don't blame you."

From there, they launched into other subjects, some as familiar and comfortable as old boots. Winterspeer's practised epistle on the farming life. Still wondering at the mechanism that allowed the urban middle class to eat well and flourish, and to even make fun of the ass-patched under-class that fed them. Wondering too at the insane commitment of those who laboured against unforgiving earth and climate, and equally unforgiving banks. He presented his theory, only slightly revised with the years, that the earth was planning a great revenge on those who practised intensive farming techniques and, worse yet, genetic engineering.

"Man will outwit himself as always. You make a turkey with an ever larger breast, a veritable mountain of meat out of every bird body. But what do you get in the end? A turkey that cannot fuck!"

Sheila's voice from the kitchen: "Walter, for heaven's sake! Tom's not asleep yet; I know he's listening at the crack."

Winterspeer told of his sadnesses. That still his poetry went unpublished. "I heard on CBC Radio (so it must be true) that the era of the alcoholic writer has passed. The public has rejected it, pronounced the perceptions of the drunken mind to be of interest no longer. At first, this did not trouble me. I could go back to marijuana in a pinch. But then, this smooth Upper Canadian went on to say that he believed Canada's youth was discovering sobriety and fitness, the bell-like perceptions of the clear mind, its thoughts nourished by the well-oiled workings of the healthy body. I saw rows and rows of shiny-faced blond children in uniforms, Gabriel. I saw doom for Winterspeer, literary and literal."

Gabriel surprised himself by asking about Jennifer. "She's still here," Winterspeer said, then seemed reluctant to say more. Finally, "The day you brought her out, shortly before you left altogether, proved to be a beginning of sorts. She's become a regular visitor. A favourite friend to us both, which is amazing — it's always been so difficult for anyone to befriend both Sheila and myself. Jennifer has managed it. I told her, early on, that she could have the run of the place for her plant research. Actually, I told her that if she managed to uproot every plant on the farm and thus render the land a desert, she'd do me a favour. She did come out most weekends and Sheila started going with her. Between them, they are approaching total knowledge of everything that roots and crawls on Plantation Winterspeer."

"What did you talk about?"

"With me, Jennifer has the other thing, the exile thing, I guess you could call it. Not unlike what brought you here when things started to sour for you locally. She and I sit and sip, and fulminate about the great world of culture we imagine we once inhabited and perversely left; we bitch about the abundant lacks of this place. That sort of thing."

"Does she mention my name?" A line from a Lightfoot song and an old shared joke. Winterspeer lit fresh cigarettes for himself and Gabriel before answering.

"No, she doesn't. But if it's any consolation, I suspect she thinks of you and doesn't mention you deliberately."

"I'd be happy if she didn't think about me at all."

Winterspeer was suddenly serious, uncharacteristically so, even a bit angry. He lunged forward and squinted at Gabriel through his smoke.

"Two things of great importance, Gabriel. What you said there is a lie, not that I judge you for it, but you should know. And, second, don't pity her whatever you do. Don't diminish her that way. Jennifer is strong, the worthy object of worship — she certainly has mine. She is not one to cherish pain, so if she does think about you it must be for the pleasure of it." Winterspeer sat back, physically relenting. "Then again, I may be wrong. Admiration distorts. You always wore one another well, I thought."

"We wore one another out."

"Oh well, so be it then. Life fails art again."

Walter asked Gabriel to stay. Gabriel said no. He was anxious to be outside where a great silence had taken the place of the storm. Walter followed him to the porch.

"I feel I should tell you there's a rumour that your father's trouble is more than a broken leg. Probably without foundation, but the suggestion is that he passed out on his horse, fell off with his boot still in the stirrup, and so broke his leg."

"Drunk?"

"The rumour says, sober."

Beyond Walter's porch, Gabriel entered a quiet luminous place. The wind with its final fury had blown the storm clouds off the horizon. The revealed sky contained a three-quarter moon and a leaping sheen of northern lights. The night felt immense, grew bigger with each step away from other lights. All this had been there, thought Gabriel, was always there above the storms.

The lacy swells in the north sky struck him as completely feminine, as if some dancer swirled a veil, tossed it to the roof of the sky, drew it down. Walking in the deep snow with his head tipped back, he didn't feel drunk anymore, the booze having nothing to butt against. A moment of silver lust. His mind groped back through a series of images, the women he had known, each held up to this lady of the sky, and discarded.

Until Jennifer.

Holding Jennifer up proudly, he aimed into the centre of the swirling veil and and continued to make his mark on the untracked snow.

6

Gabriel and Jennifer Owchenko met first as pupil and teacher in St. Thomas Aquinas High School, Beaver Creek. She arrived at St. Tom's to teach biology and chemistry when Gabriel was in grade twelve. She was the first young and pretty teacher he had ever seen.

One noon hour, when Gabriel was leaning against the lockers with Dalton and Jimmy, and Miss Owchenko swayed past them up the hall, the words "ripe fruit" came suddenly out of Jimmy's mouth. Gabriel envied Jimmy for thinking and saying it because it really was the perfect description for a woman so full-breasted and full-hipped, for someone with such soft lips and large green eyes. Gabriel could imagine her as fruit, so ripe it was about to slip off the stem by its own full weight.

This strange situation of having a desirable teacher drove Gabriel and his friends to pranks. They stole a fetal pig from a jar in Miss Owchenko's lab and put a Mecanno set electric motor inside it. By belts and axles, and metal struts fixed inside the legs, they turned it into a kind of vehicle. Behind her back, they released it up the aisle and, when the screaming subsided, Miss Owchenko almost magically knew who to blame. She had the three of them suspended from school for two weeks.

Gabriel spent this time studying her subjects harder than he had ever studied anything before. Ironically, it was how he discovered he could learn such things easily, that he particularly enjoyed chemistry. On the next set of exams, after he came back to school, Gabriel beat everyone by several marks. But, in the half of his dream he couldn't control, he was disappointed. He got a slightly startled green-eyed look from Miss Owchenko when she handed back his first successful exam but she didn't seem to notice, or certainly did not acknowledge, his calf stares of worship — right up to the day when the double doors of St. Tom's clanked shut behind him for the last time.

Gabriel forgot about Miss Owchenko then. A kid's crush for a teacher — it was an embarrassing thing, childish, something with no place in the tough, adult world he saw himself as now inhabiting. He did hear of her from time to time, rumours mostly; the ones started by spurned beaus that she was frigid or lesbian, and the other set that said she was fucking everything in pants. The people who, like the press, saw it as their duty to move information, circulated both rumours, easily tolerant of the contradictions.

At home, Hank talked about her too; called her the "crazy school marm from town" who went around digging up perfectly ordinary plants and putting them in bags. She took pictures of the ground!

Guess you needed a university education to take pictures of dirt.

It was around then that Dalton, Jimmy and Gabriel were swearing their oath in the Queen Elizabeth tavern, and shortly before the time that their rodeoing turned into the high stakes game of joust. Then, in quick order, Gabriel's neck sent a hot wire to his brain, Hank threw him off the place, and Gabriel went to work at the gas plant — the same gas plant he and his friends had always scorned as too boring, safe and low-paying for them.

In the bank one Friday afternoon near Christmas, Gabriel was waiting to cash a paycheque when the woman in front of him turned and he saw it was Miss Owchenko. There was a winter indoor rodeo on in the town arena that day and the bank was almost empty. Gabriel and Miss Owchenko were having to wait anyway because an old man in front of them was demanding that the only teller produce his last month's cheques. They were forced to talk. Gabriel had changed, she said. She hadn't, he replied, meaning a compliment but almost certainly conveying something else. Why wasn't he at the rodeo, she asked; wasn't that one of his big interests? Not anymore, he said and added, "People change."

How it came up he wasn't sure but he asked her if she wanted to go for a beer. She said she'd rather not. Her students had the afternoon off for the rodeo and were probably in the bar. She didn't want to embarrass them. But they could go to her place and have a drink there.

And so it began. The one drink turned into several and that, by quick but complicated turns, gave rise to a decision to go to Lethbridge for the evening, the nearest city, sixty miles away. Coming out of a Chinese restaurant after supper there, Jennifer — Miss Owchenko no longer — coaxed him across the street into the downtown park where, like children, they started playing hide and seek among the drunks and trees. Next thing they were climbing a tree next to a fenced train engine. From the first crotch of branches, they saw the policeman coming. He told them to get the hell down. Jennifer teased him. Is there a tree-climbing by-law in Lethbridge, she asked? And while they jawed back and forth, Gabriel slid down so the join of branch and tree held them together, flush, like doubling on a short-backed horse. Before they climbed down, she slid her arms back and spread her fingers over his thighs. He let his face down into the coarse swarm of her hair.

They wound up spending the weekend in a Lethbridge motor hotel. On Saturday, Jennifer led them on a buying spree around town. They bought swimming trunks for the hotel pool; she bought him the first sports jacket he had ever owned. When they got back to Beaver Creek, he did not leave her basement suite. He moved in and stayed for most of the next eight months.

This caused a scandal around town, and came close to costing Jennifer her job. The heat between them kept her from caring much about that. She even found ways to ignore it when students in her class made cracks out loud behind her back, replaying what they heard at home. The other teachers drifted away, even while their union was battling the school board on her behalf. The union won but she hardly noticed. She wasn't a civil rights activist, she told herself, just a victim of love.

But, somewhere along the line — in Gabriel — a different kind of itch began. Studying for his steam engineering certificate in their quiet isolated evenings, every problem was worked out to choruses of what his bosses were telling him at the plant. They said he could go to university, that he had "what it takes." Hell, he could come back some day and run a plant like this. While he studied and thought these things through, Jennifer made a poncho for him out of raw wool on her loom. The rack and slam of her weaving became, for him, the sound of guilt.

As more time went by, they did talk about it and, when they did, Gabriel bent things. He twisted the conversation so Jennifer, as his one-time teacher, was trapped into agreeing with his bosses about university. Put that way, she had to agree even though both knew the longing in Gabriel was as much for new horizons — including new women — as it was for higher education. Looking for an easy way out he suggested they both could use a fresh start. She should go somewhere too. At this, her anger was sudden and immense.

"Don't presume to fix my life, you twerp."

When the papers came from the university, a better time arrived with them. There was no point arguing now. Jennifer helped him fill out the forms; Gabriel sent them; they passed what remained of the summer in peace.

Then finally, he was packing. They stood beside the pick-up, a few boxes in back, the sports jacket and a couple of pressed shirts on a hanger in the cab. The wind ripped their hair, flapped their clothes, seemed impatient to have Gabriel in its grip.

"At least you won't look like a complete bumpkin."

"How's that?"

She nodded toward the sports jacket.

"I'd feel stupid wearing it."

She laughed. "I guess trying to civilize you was a losing proposition from the start."

A half-hearted embrace, pale shadow of so many better ones. She swung away and down the steps. Gabriel felt sorrow then. To see her disappear down, as if into a hole. But, in the truck, driving east, then north, happiness swept all that aside. He reared back and sang his cowboy songs.

7

Ten thousand. That was roughly the number of students at the University of Calgary in Gabriel's first year. And half of them women. Walking around during frosh week, giving savage looks at anyone who approached him with a pile of beanies, Gabriel couldn't have been much more impressed. Women of every race on earth, about one in five of them pretty. His only loyalty to Jennifer was that he never compared her. She was undeniably fine; more so or less than all these campus co-eds was something he tried not to consider.

As a student of engineering, Gabriel soon realized he wasn't going to see much of these women. He spent most of his time stuck in the engineering building, an all-male enclave stranded apart from the other campus buildings like some kind of monastery, a mad monastery where the monks all wanted miserably to fail at chastity. Horny in an adolescent fashion, they reminded Gabriel of a herd of yearling steers, humping away at anything with a back, going through the motions with no hope of satisfaction. Between and even during their orgies of work, they spoke a language awkwardly stuffed with visions of spread-eagled women. The horniness spilled over into pranks, artless practical jokes and petty vandalisms that brought groans of embarrassment from the rest of the campus. The other students made fun of them, called them "plumbers." The word engineer itself became a term of insult. "You're acting like an engineer."

Gabriel went along with it for the first year. He wanted to fit in, was somewhat desperate himself. Naughty newsletters, stag parties with movies from Sweden, exotic dancers hired to celebrate the end of a tough set of exams, hookers they claimed to go to (who, in fact, they just talked to on downtown street corners and were mercilessly teased by) — Gabriel followed at a slight distance but would have defended it all if pressed. All the same, by the end of first year, he had a plan for escape.

The first article of Gabriel's plan was to involve no other engineering students in it. It wasn't personal; he liked his fellow engineers and thought of them as kin. But he also knew that he could not meet the kind of women he had in mind accompanied by guys in purple and yellow football jackets. Nor could he meet them in the engineering building. The plan therefore was to take two introductory arts courses in second year, which he would go to alone and in secret.

Gabriel's Art Appreciation class commenced in September with a Canadian Literature course to follow in January. Despite his efforts to hide what he was doing, word soon got around that Gabriel was leaving the monastery at ten to two, three days a week, and was not going to the students' union building to eat cheeseburgers or play pinball. Not wanting them to spy more closely, Gabriel admitted that he was taking an arts course.

"What the Christ for?!"

He said it was to round himself out — so he wouldn't wind up an ignorant bastard like all of them. The right sort of answer but it still left some guardedness and suspicion. For the time being he was too flakey to trust. Combined with some other thing, success with a foxy lady especially, he could just as easily become their hero. But for the time being they kept a distance, which was fine with him.

What he absolutely did not want any of them to know was the last part of his plan: that, on the way to Art Appreciation class, three days a week, he always stopped at his truck, threw his jean jacket in the cab, and went the rest of the way in a sports jacket.

While deciding to take the step, Gabriel had defined a worst-case scenario: that all he would gain was an appreciation for art. For a time this seemed his lot. He found nothing hard about the course and often felt he was back in elementary school doing a particular kind of test he'd always been good at. Where does the piggy belong? In the zoo? In the mountains? On a farm? Match the pillar with the pediment and tell teacher if it's Ionic or Doric. One of these is a Vermeer, the other a Rembrandt; tell us which is which and what characteristics enabled you to choose. How many rabbits are there in this picture?

No doubt it was fun getting high marks without once having to stay up all night gripping his hair as he often did for engineering assignments, but, if you asked him in October, was the experiment a success, he would have said no. In more than a month, he had not made the acquaintance of a single woman, nor a married one, for that matter.

If there was any progress it was that his days of observation from the back of the theatre classroom had decreased his awe for the Greater Urban Female considerably. There was no doubt they were good-looking, well-dressed and well-groomed; they gleamed health and there was not a crooked tooth among them. But, every day in class, their shrill bleats of laughter and their stupid questions chipped away at the edifice of Gabriel's esteem. The men (boys, really) in these classes were no better, of course, and, when they asked their stupid questions, there was an added whine of not very dangerous rebellion. "How come there's sometimes more than one name for a kind of art — it's confusing, eh?" But Gabriel couldn't have cared less about them. It was the women he'd come looking for and it was the women who were making him wonder if his sights were set too low.

For the next month of term, Gabriel spent much time in Art Appreciation class reworking his fantasy. In its revised form, he was in pursuit of one woman, a woman he did not see anywhere around him. She would be easy to spot because she would stand so much taller than the others. A long-maned head, or maybe the hair done up tight with a few curls dangling by delicate ears. A woman who wore silk scarves tossed over a shoulder, who rode horses — and not after cows. Partial to tweeds, he suspected, and to high leather boots that gleamed.

Gabriel even went so far as to provide her with opinions on things. For example, she would like the arts, but with none of the adolescent cheerleading he heard from these other girls.

"I went to a real neat movie last night!"

"I wouldn't kick Michelangelo's David out of bed for eating crackers!" (Big bed, cold comfort.)

"Mona Lisa's so beautiful!"

As if they could overcome their ignorance with sheer enthusiasm.

His lady would have quieter reasons for liking what she liked. In his fantasy, Gabriel couldn't quite make out *what* she was saying about the arts, but she always said it to him and he always comprehended quickly and in just the right spirit.

While he was dreaming this, Gabriel had to dodge round old loyalties and bigotries — a lifetime with Dalton and Jimmy where you automatically disliked everyone who wasn't like you. People with money were first in line for this treatment: inheritors of old ranches and anyone living in a big house in town. These were accused of all sorts of crimes, but mainly sexual ones involving animals, both living and stuffed. And snobbishness; they were always snobs.

That was the sorest part now: not only was Gabriel trying to consort with these people, he wanted to become one.

On a day in early November, a curly-headed, round-faced boy-man sat down beside Gabriel in Art Appreciation class. He interrupted one of Gabriel's tweedy woman fantasies with the statement, "What I've noticed about the female figures of Renaissance art is that they're fat."

Gabriel looked over and the first thing he noticed was the guy's sports jacket. It was almost exactly like Gabriel's own.

After class, at the other's insistence, the two of them went for coffee. Over coffee, this guy — Clive was his name — too loudly outlined his plans for leaving the working class forever. His shallow ambitions seemed like caricatures of Gabriel's own and, for awhile, Gabriel had the paranoid idea that the class had put Clive up to this, that the clothes and statements had been rehearsed for Gabriel's humiliation.

Eventually, Gabriel dropped the idea. If the class were that clever he was doomed anyway.

Clive had studied the levels of female enrolment in all introductory courses. Art Appreciation was a good one, he said; its female to male ratio was among the highest. He had a second motive for taking the course and that was to learn to "talk art." You couldn't get far in any of the easy walks of life, he said, if you couldn't talk art. Clive's major was actually political science which he described as "the route of least resistance." It had the triple advantage of being easy, of being the major of at least as many women as men, and of being a tremendous ticket to an unstrenuous career in either party politics or the civil service. At worst, you could wind up in the foreign service, living well but in danger of being bombed or taken hostage.

In addition to study, Clive was pursuing his goals by belonging to political parties. He had originally belonged to the Liberal Party of Canada.

"I knew I had great potential with them because they like rags to patronage kinds of stories. Clive Ruthven, they would say, came from a family of tradesmen and small-time entrepreneurs. Salt of the earth but look at him now, by George: a successful party bagman."

Clive, however, had foreseen the Liberal comeuppance: a mighty storm on the horizon that no last minute give-away was going to blow off. With real reluctance he left the Liberal Party which had given him summer jobs, sent him to conventions, poured free drink down him. He joined the Conservatives just in time to campaign vigorously for his local candidate during the election that swept the party to power.

Clive had worried at first that it would be more difficult to rise with the Conservatives where old money was preferred to new blood. But, to get elected, the Conservatives had indulged in a lot of one-downing and, temporarily at least, guys like Clive were coming in handy. He was delegate material again: could patronage be far behind?

The cup of coffee with Clive after Art Appreciation class became a tradition, one that Gabriel looked forward to. They became friends and did things together after classes and on weekends. Being loud, a little wild-eyed, and apparently disliked by all women who had anything in common with the tweedy woman, Clive was exactly the wrong friend for Gabriel to make. But that was part of the attraction. Having made this friend, Gabriel did not feel quite as guilty of betrayal. Flying down the right wing, taking aim on the well-appointed tweed goal, Gabriel had deliberately taken a penalty behind the play; thus proving, he hoped, that he wasn't totally desperate to score.

If Clive was social ballast for Gabriel, what was Gabriel to Clive? Gabriel never lost sight of that. He would never get Clive an invitation to an embassy party, never introduce him to a rich or influential Conservative. So maybe it was the same for both of them; maybe both needed a friendship proven pure by its disadvantages.

At the end of term, Clive and Gabriel had two out of the five A's awarded by the Art Appreciation professor. Dr. Ingblom had a tradition of inviting his A students for tea and a chat in his office and Gabriel and Clive went there on the appointed day to honour the tradition. Though he allegedly wanted to get to know them better, Dr. Ingblom did all the talking in his reedy, tumbledown voice. He dropped compliments like confetti but his eyes spoke a different tale — of disappointment and annoyance. The fissured skin framing his eyes pinched and quivered and defied the worn-out speech of congratulation. Afterward, Clive and Gabriel agreed that he must have been asking himself how the hell this pair of jackasses (who he distinctly remembered talking and tittering at the back of his class) had managed to place among his A's. They also agreed that he would have settled on a charge of cheating, which in an indirect way was true.

8

After Christmas, that second year of university, Gabriel had to continue the search alone. Clive would have liked to join him but he had already taken Canadian Literature. He warned Gabriel that it was definitely harder than Art Appreciation though it had the advantage of an even higher female to male ratio.

For reasons quite muddy, especially to himself, Gabriel could not like this new course. It was irrational he knew because, right there before him, three days a week, was the closest thing to the Tweedy Woman he had ever seen on this campus.

The woman didn't actually wear tweeds but something about her long striding carriage spoke of thoroughbred horses grazing behind white fences. Her neck was the part of her that held Gabriel's attention longest during every class. It was so slim and left her shoulders at such a perfect angle. It was usually visible because she liked to wear her hair up, held by a finely tooled leather clasp, with fine golden tendrils whispering down — just as he had imagined.

Her beauty weakened Gabriel. The only time she was not at the exact forefront of his mind was when she was pushed aside by a vision of himself. These were pictures of shit-kicking cloddishness, awkward, bowlegged boorishness: more than a sports jacket could hide.

Gabriel had two main responses to this. First, he threw his sports coat into a corner of his closet and went back to wearing his jean jacket, full time. Second, he came up with a variety of reasons for hating his section of CanLit. Everything about it — the professor, the other students, the subject matter — pissed him off entirely. To an imaginary group of listeners, all engineers, he kept up a mental litany of his complaints.

Did you catch the guy with the orange brushcut and the earring? And what about the prof? Dr. Phipps, for Chrissake. The way he pinches his chin between thumb and forefinger while his pinky sticks out?

The course itself seemed to spend forever on some 19th century Englishwoman's diary, written someplace in Ontario. Gabriel refused to see why it was any different than the one anybody's auntie might write, even down to the recipes for spring salad. Dr. Phipps said it was one of the recognized roots of modern Canadian literature. God help the tree, Gabriel said to the imaginary group of engineers. Any student that shared Dr. Phipps's enthusiasm for the diary, Gabriel especially despised.

Only Clive heard any of this. When they met, Gabriel did imitations: "My Dear Harriet, I don't know how I shall continue. The wilderness of Upper Canada is scarcely to be believed. I fear I shall never be able to convert a single one of these rough, ignorant backwoods girls into a truly useful upstairs maid. Still, the forest is lovely, particularly at sunset when the cathedral spires pierce the firmament...."

Gabriel's essay on the subject was less successful. A poor mark from Dr. Phipps gave him an added reason to be embarrassed and resentful. He was certain the tweedy woman knew of his "D" and had added "dull" to the litany of his faults. He had not spoken one word to her as the calendar turned to February, nor had he said a thing in class, yet he was certain he had failed repeatedly in her eyes.

One of these failures involved her name. He had seen it written on her calf leather clipboard: Phoebe. He cherished the sound of it, had a few imaginary conversations with her, calling her by that name (conversations which of course revealed his intelligence, his sensitivity, his wit). But then, Dr. Phipps asked her one day to comment on a piece they were to have read for class and Gabriel heard a name completely different than the one in his head. Dr. Phipps had said "Fee-Bee." Feebee? The name Gabriel had been silently saying over and over was closer in sound to phobia. Even though Gabriel had never made the mistake aloud, he felt humiliated.

The course finally moved out of the 19th century. The 20th might have been pleasanter terrain for Gabriel but, by now, the wreckage of his plan and his confidence was so complete he was afraid to think, let alone speak. He passed the time studying the elegant angle at which Phoebe's neck leapt from the heart-shaped foundation of her shoulders; and the way, when she crossed her legs, that the instep of the foot she crossed over would be in a straight line with the ankle and leg.

In the rare moments when he was aware of the class, he noticed that Dr. Phipps did not like the 20th century as much as he had liked the 19th. He was off his feed for about a month and then, suddenly, was excited again, presumably because he had arrived at a place on the course outline called "Literature by and about Canada's Natives and Métis."

For the first week on this subject, Dr. Phipps mentioned no literature at all. He told stories of Native life in the distant past, vivid portrayals of peaceful tribes living in harmony with nature and with each other. All this was "before contact." Gabriel had never imagined that a word like "contact" could be negative or positive but, off Dr. Phipps's tongue, it was like "leprosy" or "Auschwitz."

Then the white man came pouring across the continent. The fiery sweep of disease, the moral decay, the liquor trade — the profound and terrible loss. Dr. Phipps was almost in tears as the week came to a close.

The following week, he launched into the literature dealing with all of this. No novel, short story or poem of it pleased him. He came back again and again to the basic inability of the white man to do justice to this great story. It awaited a great Native bard, as Ireland had awaited Joyce — with the difference that Ireland had never lost its culture to the same extent that the North American Native had.

Gabriel began to fear his emotions. As Phipps produced a series of these "White" works, showing why each was lacking in some basic, unforgivable way, Gabriel felt a new and ever stronger irritation grow. On the days between CanLit classes that week, Gabriel brooded on what he had heard, and had trouble concentrating on his other more important work. He even tried to avoid Dr. Phipps's final class on the subject but, as two o'clock Friday afternoon approached, he felt like some bully was behind him giving him shoves between the shoulder blades. And that made him madder still.

As the class began, Gabriel could tell that Dr. Phipps was raring to go. The professor criss-crossed the old terrain until he had beaten it muddy, coming always back to the theme of a White Man's inability to write on this subject.

"The White Man can never hope to penetrate the mystery of this boundless Red tragedy!"

The weight of this statement on Gabriel's thinly effaced patience finally caused it to tear. He stood beside his desk.

"You're wrong."

Phipps was surprised to see the sleeping giant wake and speak. "I'm what?"

"You say that White Men can't write about Indians, but some Indian's supposed to come along and see it all?"

Phipps made a clucking sound with his throat. "Now, excuse me. I don't believe I said anything that sweeping. The non-Native — and I wish you would say Native — I understand that Native people are quite sensitive about the word Indian — the non-Native can of course understand the surface of Native life, as I believe I have, but what I doubt is the ability to see into the heart of the matter, to truly understand the culture and the history."

Gabriel persisted. "Alright, if this tragedy is as complete as you say, and the culture is so lost, I don't see how an Indian can get at it any better, that's all."

"Native," said Phipps, allowing his impatience to show in broad ways, "how a Native can get at it. In any case I'm going to have to bring this discussion to a close because there's a lot I want to say before the end of the hour. I'm afraid you'll have to accept on faith that I'm fairly well-read in this area and that many scholars, Native and White, agree with the point of view I'm presenting."

Gabriel held the corner of his desk tightly, exerting force against a tremble in his arms and back.

"My source is as good as yours — probably better."

"I suppose we have to hear about it then."

For an instant before he spoke, Gabriel understood what he was about to do, that he couldn't say this thing without altering a pattern he had always lived by. It was too late to change direction.

"I'm half Indian — not 'Native' which sounds stupid to me. And that makes me a Halfbreed or a Breed, not a Métis. I'm not even sure what a Métis is. I don't like to make a big deal about it because I don't feel Halfbreed. I don't know any more about living in tents or hunting buffalos than you do. Less actually, because I didn't know half the stuff you said last week. The Indians around here who do know probably got it from the same books you did."

Gabriel made a gesture at the others in the class. "Most of these people probably had grandparents from Europe; if you wanted a book written about Germany, would you look for somebody in class with blond hair and say, ya, that's the guy? But when it comes to us, you think our brains are different or something. I don't like people looking at me as if I was something special."

The longest speech of Gabriel's life and, sitting down, he could feel the eyes of every person in the room looking at him, "as if he were something special." And whose fault was it? Not the professor's. Not the students'. The adrenalin of the moment began to subside and, behind it, came a thick disgust. He realized that Dr. Phipps was talking to him and that he'd missed most of it.

"...can't say that you've changed my opinion, but you certainly have given us something important to consider in this analysis. Perhaps we could hear more from you another time. Thank you. Thank you very much."

Gabriel forced his eyes up from the floor. He looked at Dr. Phipps. At all the other faces, facing him. At Phoebe. A slim forefinger lay next to her neck, the line in perfect parallel, the long fingernail pointing to her mouth which formed a smile. Gabriel knew then that he had been wrong to think she had noticed anything about him during the past months. But now, because he was a Halfbreed, she had.

Gabriel went out with Phoebe for three weeks. Much of their time together was spent in the students' union cafeteria, drinking coffee.

And smoking. Gabriel, who smoked only occasionally, smoked all the time with Phoebe so that he could watch her. She took all the cigarettes he offered, and she hated every one. She fought the smoke, tried to blow or wave it away so it didn't smell up her hair and clothing, or, God forbid, get in her lungs.

In the first of these conversations over coffee they established that Gabriel was an engineering student who hoped to run gas plants someday, perhaps even to design and build them. Phoebe was an English major who wasn't sure what she wanted to do afterward.

"I'm surprised you're going to be an engineer. That's what my dad does."

He stopped himself short of saying there wasn't much call for buffalo hunters these days. "It's just what I'm good at," he said.

He asked her, why English.

"I like to read."

"Maybe you could be a proofreader at a newspaper."

He'd meant it as a joke but she didn't seem to notice. Careers were serious business.

"They work at night, don't they?"

"I don't know. I guess so."

"I don't think I could work at night."

Envious boys streamed by their table. Inevitably, one of them was Clive. It was Gabriel's fourth time sitting in the cafeteria with Phoebe and Clive had not yet heard any mention of this new development in his friend's life. Clive didn't wait for an invitation; he sat down on Phoebe's side of the table and began straightaway to talk.

"Phoebe. Great name. Latin, the sun. Phoebus in *The Hunchback of Notre Dame*. I always thought I'd make a good Phoebus. What do you think? Did you notice my radiance?"

Clive had his usual effect. She looked nervous, embarrassed. Her body tilted away from him, yearned for wings. Clive kept talking and worked his arm up on the chairback behind her.

The next time Clive met Gabriel, he wasn't angry about the secrecy. If there was one thing in the world Clive respected it was deceit.

"But how? How did you do it? There's a trick, isn't there? And now that you know, you won't tell me. That's fair. Otherwise it wouldn't be a trick and everybody would have a beautiful, upper class girlfriend. Cripes! Just think of the gorgeous rich girlfriends she must have!"

Gabriel had no intention of telling Clive the secret.

After their second night out — the movies, a pizza — Phoebe and Gabriel went back to her apartment and made love. It was done in a polite, understated way; controlled and unspectacular. She conducted him like an orchestra of one. "Easy." "Wait, wait." "Okay now." His impulse to thrust — the basis of pleasure, he thought — seemed out of place here, crass like the rooting of an animal. She wanted things to stay within limits, to stop before anyone cried out loud, definitely before sweat.

All this time she hadn't said anything about his being a Halfbreed but he remained convinced she was dying to, that that desire alone accounted for everything. After several more evenings and nights in bed, two weeks' worth, it happened. In the quiet moments after equally quiet sex, she asked him about being Métis. He exploded. He realized as he was doing it that he had been waiting all along to rage at her this way, and how unfair it was.

"You're not fucking Tonto, you know!"

She began to cry.

"There hasn't been a feather in my family's hair for about a century but you're dying to stick one there, aren't you?"

"I'm only interested," she sobbed. "It's not fair to hate me for being interested."

The tweedy woman fantasy came to an end. The only aftermath was that Phoebe dropped out of Canadian Literature, and that Clive, meeting her awhile later and probably not by accident, winkled out of her the reason for the romance's sudden demise. "What an ace!" he told Gabriel over the phone that night. "If I was a Métis I could be Prime Minister in under a decade. You lucky bastard. You sly dog. Here I thought you'd done it by finesse and all along it was genetic advantage."

"Clive. Shut up. I never want to talk about this again so shut up."

"Okay. That's fair."

BAPTISTE   Where the buffalo roam

9

The municipal snowplow: a square maw chewing the drifts and spitting them in an unending side spew. Carving squares on an aerial surface of white. Reinstating a checkerboard notion of civilization.

By the time the plow worked its way around the curve of Baptiste's hill and down into the farmyard, things between Gabriel and Lyla had settled. The day after their argument they had worked together under a hot spring sun. They pumped water, tossed out the last of the black cores of hay, heeled and doped calves, broke a trail to the bale pile — hours of sweat that justified silence.

That night, it was more difficult. In the kitchen and living room, they moved around one another like ions bearing the same charge, too polite in the way they shared the space. Silence seemed like aggression here so they spoke; of horses, cows, crops — subjects free of polarity. The only reference to Hank was in the language of knitting needles, Lyla's hands whipping wool into pieces of sweater the Old Man's size. Still, if the picture of his mother hadn't been missing from the piano top, Gabriel might have passed the evening with a quiet mind.

When the snowplow had come and gone, and a gash of road split the snow like some Bible picture of the Red Sea parted, Lyla went to the house and changed into town clothes. She became again the womanly figure Gabriel had discovered in his father's bed, a transformation that aged her. He remembered thinking that first night that she must be around fifty. He had been revising that estimate down ever since. Now, seeing her in makeup, white blouse and pink western suit, he wondered if fifty wasn't low.

Gabriel rode with her to the place where he had left his truck during the storm. The drift was gone, shot through the belly of the plow, and his truck stood alone, slewed sideways, as if a drunk had run out of gas without the sense to coast to the shoulder.

When he entered the kitchen again, something about the silence reminded Gabriel that he was alone. He considered diving into the cupboards and corners in search of memory, but this desire had drifted with the storm. He pulled a chair out onto the step and leaned it back so the midday sun shone on his face. A mild spring warmth, and a light that painted the inside of his closed eyelids gold crimson. Water gurgled in the eaves, dripped through rusted holes in the troughs, drummed the ground from one end of the house to the other.

It was the kind of moment (he recognized it from a few he'd had before) when the farming life appealed. Was there anyone anywhere as free as a farmer on a day like this when the work was done? It was a peace purchased with bull work, but at least the farmer chose it. The contract was in that way pure and something Gabriel sensed in advance he would never know trading on the parchment square he'd finally earned from the university.

His mind warmed in the sun. His thoughts ran.

Farming. He wondered if he could do it. He had most of the tools, the ones you need to fix a tractor or an implement torn apart by the collision of dirt and steel. He had the brains to plan a cycle of seed, weed and harvest, to breed for a better herd of cattle. But that was only the edge. To go around and around the perimeter of a field with nothing to show for each hour but another hundred feet of chewed earth, sliced crop, separated seed, you needed something else; whatever that something was, you had to have it, for, without it, you would start to shrink faster than the untilled portion of your field.

Sun drunk, Gabriel even felt he might share that lonely quality with the stunt and thickened men of his childhood. City people always asked the same question: if it wasn't an awfully boring life. Farmers never knew how to answer. Gabriel imagined speaking on behalf of them: it's also boring to breathe. Why not see the same necessity in a blade cutting down another round of wheat?

Then his thoughts took a tumble. The tripwire as always Hank. Hank. Gabriel opened his eyes and stared up where the road became visible at the hill's edge. Right then, he expected to see the four-wheel drive rumble into view. The fruity conversation of birds came to his ears, the drumming of water, the slow luffing of sheets Lyla had hung on the clothes line. The road stayed empty.

Cruel now, mutinous, in the grip of feelings he hadn't known since the last time he lived here, Gabriel called up Walter's words of a few nights before. More wrong with Hank than a broken leg. Maybe the old horse *was* dying then, and maybe he would not live to come down that hill again. The thought brought Gabriel no sorrow; no real comfort either. The old arguments swirling with the dust inside the house, the sour memories rising with the frost each spring. Hank would always be here somewhere.

Gabriel stood up, searched the yard, the sad round-shouldered buildings. He cursed it all. If that's the way it was, he thought, if the Old Man had made this place so no one else could live here ... then maybe the fitting end had already been spelled. Doors and windows plucked out, a socketed skull humming tunes when the chinooks blew. The place would pass into other hands and some busy farmer would plow up the last of the native grass, the sweet meadows soon to purple with shooting stars. He would never know, nor care if he did know, that the bones of Baptiste were sewn under the brow of the east hill, that a dark woman used to pick spring bouquets and summer berries on the hill to the west. The busy farmer would plow out those memories without a care.

In the end, he would push these shacks and coops into a pile and set them on fire, maybe that night telling his wife that the foolish bastards that used to live here had built on the only fertile acre the farm had.

10

Lyla returned to the farm an hour after sunset. She was by herself. The power company had been out to hook up the line that afternoon and, by the unflattering light from the naked kitchen bulb, Gabriel could see that she'd been crying as she drove. Without answering his hello she went back to the bedroom and stayed there for most of the evening. Gabriel thought he heard her move into the living room around ten.

All through this, Gabriel stayed at the kitchen table. He was playing solitaire with a soiled and warped deck of cards. He never won so maybe, like the song, he was "playing solitaire 'til dawn with a deck of fifty-one." He couldn't be bothered to check. Counting flowers on the wall — except there weren't any. He could count plaster cracks and water stains and kill time that way if he liked.

Lost in the boredom of the game, he nudged thoughts around and arrived at the same conclusion from several directions. When an afternoon in the sun had him considering the farming life, it was time to move on. Definitely time. The problem was that he had things to settle first. When he answered this call, there had been nothing. Now there was. That was the cost of coming here.

Ever since he was a kid and some teacher had used balls and a flashlight to explain the comings and goings of the earth and other planets, Gabriel had thought of his own family in these terms. In the centre (the undisputed centre after Baptiste died) was Hank, the fiery star that would burn you good if you got too close. His mother and Joe were the planets. She orbited too near, was never safe, while Joe kept his distance — circling as far back as he could without losing the anchor of gravity. Joe: a dark, cold, silent planet; the kind without water or air that you know cannot support life.

Gabriel never saw himself as a planet. He was more of a comet, like Halley's; his orbit at once obeying and defying the sun. Every once in a long while he roared through the heart of the system causing a stir. It wasn't a very accurate way of describing his place in the family, but it was his fantasy and he gave himself a showy place in it.

When he was eleven, the system heaved. His mother lost momentum. Tired of going round, she fell into the fire and, when she did, one of those equal and opposite thrusts the universe is programmed for kicked him right out the other side. It took years to happen but that was how he preferred to see the cause and its effect.

Then: his five years of freedom. His image of the system over that period — when he bothered to think of it at all — was fixed. Sun and dark planet, unchanging. The fact was, Gabriel wanted it to be incapable of change. It couldn't threaten him then and he could safely take his eye away.

But it had changed. Joe's not being here was proof. How the sun's pull must have weakened to free up that feeble, clinging planet. Gabriel's understanding of the system ended there. For one thing, *he* was also back and he was not sure why. More important, if he moved the balls, shifted the planets, where should Lyla go?

Gabriel looked at the cards and noticed that he had lost again. He drew them into a pile, faces up, faces down, the bowed sides opposing. Mixed up like that, the cards looked like more than one deck's worth. Only prior knowledge could tell you it was one. How to win at solitaire with a short deck? How to put this puny planetary system together without knowledge of how its planets now behaved?

He stared at the wall above the stove and noticed in a new way the crucifix that hung there. A braided palm dangled from it like a scrotum. Every Palm Sunday his mother had brought her palm back from church, split out the leaves and braided it. She tied it there. And there the last one hung because of some crazy acceptance of familiar things. A palm in a house where God hadn't been feared for five seconds in fifteen years. It would serve everyone right if it disintegrated onto a lit burner.

On the other side of the wall: Lyla — knitting her thoughts together, Hank back to health. An act like prayer. The last thing Gabriel wanted was any part of Lyla's sadness tonight; he was sure the feeling was mutual. But was there any other way? If he wanted to sail out of this system and think of it as little as he had before, there were things within that circle of sadness he had to know.

Filling two cups with swarthy coffee, Gabriel stepped through the arch. In the low wattage gloom of waxy shades, she sat. The hands, inert when he first appeared, started at once to mince the knitting needles. He set a cup on the flat arm of her chair. Sat close by. She crossed her legs the other way so they pointed toward the piano.

"Look, I'm not going to pretend I care more about all this than I do."

"Nice way to begin. Why don't you not bother, period." She knit faster.

"I can't make plans until I know."

She slammed the knitting down. "Know *what*? I don't feel like confiding in you one damn bit."

"Then don't. All I want to know is what's going on with Hank. And whether Joe's coming back."

"The answer is, I don't bloody know. How the hell would I know where Joe took his jail bait and what his plans are? I'm not the lost and found."

Gabriel had the sudden feeling they were on different topics. "What are you talking about?"

Lyla jerked her head around his way, sorrow and amusement forming an ugly crossbred emotion across her face. "He didn't tell you when he phoned?" She read his look, snorted. "That's rich. Well, I'll enjoy telling you this. Your brother's been after Christoff's daughter down the road for months. Like a dog in heat. Day before you came, the two of them lit out on his motorcycle and haven't been seen since. Old Christoff is out looking and, frankly, if he finds them, Joe'll be a nutless wonder."

Gabriel had to laugh. There was only one Christoff girl — he didn't remember her first name — pudgy and taciturn, alone in a seat on the school bus. She'd smelled of rotten food because she horded lunch leftovers in her book bag. And the idea of Joe a-courting. Preening in front of his tin mirror, slicking back his hair. What did he do to woo her? Leave bloodied moose antlers on her step?

Then off into the night on his Harley. With the Old Man in hospital and a storm coming. All heart, Joe.

"As for your father," Lyla went on, "they think he had a heart attack. I'm taking him to Calgary for tests on Tuesday. Satisfied?" Gabriel didn't answer and she added, "I thought you might be."

She reached and touched her forehead lightly, spread her fingers out across it to shield her eyes.

"Oh, Christ. Forget I said that. Whatever reason, I guess you're here. If you'd stay until we get back it would help."

11

Lyla took Hank to Calgary on the first Tuesday in May. In the afternoon of that day, a chinook boiled up out of the mountains. Peeled of rain over the Continental Divide, it exploded onto the foothills, warm and dry. The soggy drifts of snow shrank into themselves and gave up streams of run-off as if a sponge had been wrung.

The chinook arch hung over Gabriel's head, a dense band of wind-groomed cloud following the curve of the sky from north to south. Between the cloud and the mountains: a pale blue path of cleared out sky. One of those things like northern lights that Gabriel had seen and measured by all his life but couldn't have explained. It was a pattern whose meaning was wind; and it was a kind of wind that threw stones, ripped shingles, made wearing a hat an art like the juggler's. Unaccustomed skin burned and bruised in it. It gave the locals (in jest) a westward lean and (in truth) a squint so tight against dust that your memory of them was of faces without eyes.

The day unsettled Gabriel strangely. The wind seemed to be blowing straight through his skull. The confidence he'd felt sitting in the sun a few days ago weakened steadily now. It quivered in the wind, trembled on a thin stalk. He did his work quickly and went to the house, hoping to escape. But the wind creaked the rafters, rattled the dry-puttied windowpanes, shook at him still.

Through the grimed window, laced every few seconds by a toss of grit, he watched. Past a long-dead plant in a rust coloured pot, his eyes travelled from foot to peak of the hill to the west, then back to the bottom and slowly up again. If the other hill, the east one that held his grandfather's bones, was Baptiste's Hill, then the one he stared at was Gabriel's. He'd staked his early claim climbing it as a boy, feeling victory along its brow. Then, like some fasting Indian, he'd gone there to wait for manhood. Solitary vigil: biding time until the Old Man came and ran him off. But the hill still felt like his.

An hour before sunset, Gabriel left the house. Against the wind he climbed. And, as he climbed, his mind played tricks. Instead of his own voice, he heard his father's. Cursing as he doubtless had the day he'd climbed here after his son. Gabriel could feel the anger rise, felt even the stiffness in his side where a renegade horse had rolled over the Old Man. "God-cursed, half-broke, broom-tail cayuse!"

Gabriel looked up and imagined a son sitting there, above in the dusk; smug, maybe even laughing at the sight of his stupid Old Man staggering up. "No fucking boardinghouse," he rehearsed. "No lazy half-Indian sonofabitch going to sit around here getting fed for nothing." "My farm, by Christ, and no young pup. . . . "

Then, at the summit, the real argument had begun. Gabriel cutting it short, saying, "I'll go. I don't give a shit." And Hank replying, "You're goddamn right you will."

Gabriel had strode fast down the hill ahead of his father. Straight to the grain truck and out to the field where Joe was combining. He'd driven the truck in under the auger; Joe had thrown the switch so the winter wheat spewed in. And so on through the evening and night until the combine ate the last skip of windrow in the centre of the field. With the final hopper load twirling into the box, Joe stayed in the combine cab and Gabriel in the truck.

Back at the house, Hank was long gone to town. Gabriel stuffed what things he wanted into his duffle bag. He paused in the living room to peer at the shapes of pictures and trophies on the piano top. In the kitchen, Joe was eating cold beef with his fingers. He kept his head down over the food showing Gabriel only the burl of his black head hair swirled into crazy knots by sweat inside his cap. Gabriel stood beside his little brother and offered his hand. Joe shook it without looking up.

When he reached the crest of the hill, an even stronger blast of wind slammed and almost lifted Gabriel. It rattled his jacket halves. He crossed the hilltop to the shallow mark before the fissured outcrop. Like a bone sticking out of shoulder flesh. He sat where he'd always sat, leaned back into the prickling edge and watched the sun inch toward the mountains. The rock wall lost definition; its colour deepened into silhouette. A spray of gold outlined the shadow mass and, higher up the sky, a blush of pink bled into blue.

The changes worked a burr of sadness back and forth in Gabriel. The cup of rock, the wind wedging past him, streaming off his ears. Absolutely alone.

When the last arc of the sun disappeared, the lonely sadness blasted up in him so strong it broke surface wildly. Every shade of deepening dark — the blue into navy, the pink into crimson, the mixture of the two into lilac — darkened the shade within him. What was left of the sun-warm certainty twisted and twisted in the wind until the pod of it cracked off, burst, dissipated.

That he could be alone here and happy. . . . What a joke.

Back inside the farmhouse, the whisky bottle at the end of one arm, Gabriel marched a track from the living room to the kitchen wall where the telephone hung. Each time, nearing the telephone, the loneliness drove a current down into his fingers but he did not reach for it. The one kind of help for a night like this one, but why would she? He'd given her plenty of reasons why not.

Finally, tired and starting to feel drunk, he collapsed into a chair. He stood the bottle on his knee and thought, "This feeling, whatever it is, will probably pass with the wind." He was not consoled. What if the wind didn't stop? He would be crazy then. Pure and simple. The margin so slim you had to wonder if it was worth trying. He looked from the telephone to the palm on the crucifix and wondered one more thing: whether these were his mother's thoughts toward the end. Or had she kept a quiet mind while the wind pushed her there?

You learn through practice to be alone and then the wind, in a single night, teaches you that you cannot bear it. Leaving you the choice of telephones or madness, roads or suicide. But the wind is sly. It also shows you the thinness of those bands of comfort. Says: you can talk to people, drink with people, even share their beds. But can you trust enough to hand yourself over? Can you ever learn not to be alone?

"I can't believe you have no interest in your family."

The words of Jeffery Phipps, PhD, the night Gabriel joined him for a quiet beer in a lounge near the university. Not the first time Phipps had asked but the first time Gabriel had been unable to say no.

It was still the spring of Gabriel's second year, two weeks after he had ended his romance with Phoebe and two days after he had handed in his final Canadian Literature term paper to Dr. Phipps. Phipps had given Gabriel an opportunity no other student was offered and that was to ignore the list of topics. If he liked, he could follow up in fuller form his views on Native and Métis literature.

Gabriel had been enraged at first — treat the Halfbreed different, as usual — but, when he sat down to do it, the paper Phipps wanted was the one that kept forming in his head.

In the lounge, as empty and bleary a place as Gabriel had ever seen, with imitation horse brasses on the walls and imitation muskets crossed over an imitation fireplace, Phipps made no mention of "how" Gabriel's paper was written. It was the message he'd been after and it was the message he'd dragged Gabriel out to discuss.

"I can hardly dispute your experience," Phipps said. He was rolling his cigarette filter back and forth between thumb and forefinger. "And I have to concede at least one major point that you make."

"Which one?"

"About assimilation. I believe you're right when you say that we — I'm not sure who I mean by we, white liberals, I guess — we *do* talk a lot about assimilation of Native people without, apparently, believing what we say. As you point out, we must have it lodged in our heads that assimilation can't be total, and that it can always be reversed given the right government program. You've just about convinced me that cases of total, irreversible assimilation do exist."

Gabriel imagined himself up and running around the room, whooping, "I exist! I exist!"

Phipps stopped, struggled with his cigarette, his thoughts. He threw some beer into his mouth, leaving a glisten of froth in his sketchy moustache.

"But the other things you say I find much harder to accept. For instance, this business of having no interest in your family. That strikes me, frankly, as being contrary to human nature — if you don't mind my saying so."

All these franklys and if you don't minds. Why couldn't these guys just talk? Still, Gabriel did not feel as hostile toward Phipps as he'd intended to. Earnest, troubled, trying hard to understand what might be beyond him or anyone to understand — who could hate a guy for that? In fact, Phipps seemed so upset by it all that Gabriel found himself thinking of ways to soften the blow.

"Ya, maybe I pushed too hard to make my point," he said.

Phipps made a short lunge across the table. "In what way?"

"As long as my mother and her father were around, I suppose it made some difference to me. Kids don't have much else to think about but their families. I guess I was no different."

"Tell me about them." Phipps sounded like a genial talk show host, but unprofessionally excited.

"They were pretty close to the real article, I guess you'd say. Real live Halfbreeds. They thought of themselves that way. My grandfather, Baptiste, homesteaded the farm I grew up on, which I gather wasn't that typical for a Halfbreed to do, and he didn't see much of his relations except the odd wedding. But I always had the impression he felt close to it all."

"How was he typical then?"

"Maybe I'm wrong, maybe he wasn't. What I mean is the way he talked — a little French, a little Indian. He had an old vest with flowers sewn on it. He could Red River jig. And he had this old horn pipe that he smoked sometimes. It was his father's and had some kind of battle scene scratched into it."

Phipps leaned forward again, planted his elbows in the condensation puddles on the varnished wood.

"God, that's exciting, Gabriel! It could have been the confrontation at Red River in 1869, or the insurrection of 1885 — or one of the prairie battles against the Sioux. Grand Coteau, perhaps."

"Or the battle of Jack Smith's still — I mean, we'll never know."

"Why? Don't you have the pipe?"

"We buried it with him — and I'm not going to dig it up."

Phipps looked hurt again, chain-smoking away in self-murderous fashion. Gabriel relented a little. He decided to tell the professor the kind of story he assumed he was after.

"We buried Baptiste in the hill east of the house. He asked to be sunk in there standing up so he could survey the valley, face the sunset and so on. My parents fought like hell about it. The Old Man said it was superstitious horseshit that would get us in trouble with the Mounties. Can't have a private graveyard or something. But we did it."

"That's wonderful."

"I guess. Didn't seem so at the time since it was my brother Joe and I did most of the digging. Seven-foot hole straight down. We dug for days and finally the Old Man had to use...."

"How tall was your grandfather?"

Gabriel looked at Phipps and had to laugh.

"What's so funny?"

"Just, I could see you imagining some giant of the plains. Baptiste was really short. I was almost as tall when I knew him and I was just a kid. The Old Man wanted the hole that deep to make sure Baptiste wouldn't erode out some spring. Anyway, to put an end on it, the Mounties came out, the Old Man told them this story about how Baptiste had wandered off into the mountains and never came back. So the Mounties went out with dogs and searched for him. Every night the Old Man took up a bucket of horseshit and spread it on the grave."

Finishing, Gabriel was a little pleased with himself, with the diplomacy of having told this story. But, far from being tickled and making notes, the professor was slugging out his cigarette in the glass ashtray.

"You've made a fool of me," he said.

Gabriel folded his arms tightly, sat back.

"How's that?"

"All that eloquent business in your paper about assimilation, and a wall between past and present — and then this! A really beautiful story about the family history you purport not to care about. I realize concerned white liberals, especially professors, are figures of general fun, but, frankly, I do not appreciate being made...."

"I wasn't finished."

Phipps slumped against the corrugated plastic of the seat back.

"If you remember I said at the start I was kind of interested then. But all that happened when I was nine. Kids have other things to do than sit around remembering people who are dead. My grandfather had nothing to do with how I grew up."

"What about your mother?"

"I don't want to talk about her."

Phipps nodded quickly, too quickly as if he'd understood something. Anger began to flare in Gabriel, partly at Phipps but mostly at himself for agreeing to come in the first place. He should have known that, if he started out in this direction, the trail led here.

"You wouldn't like the story," Gabriel said, his voice closed down to a single note. "Not very picturesque."

"I'm sorry. I'm not following you."

"It doesn't do much good to know how to cook and sew like a Halfbreed, does it, if nobody wants you to?"

"But," said Phipps. The hair on Gabriel's nape tickled. "But you do have a sense of loss about all this. To me that contradicts the thesis of your paper."

"Okay, fine, it's contradicted. You win."

Phipps apologized again. Gabriel wouldn't have minded hitting him.

"Let's wind this up," he said. "I didn't bullshit you. I believe what I wrote."

Gabriel pulled his wallet out of a back pocket. Phipps dove and grasped the bill. Gabriel ignored him; laid a fin on the table, stood, pulled his jacket on.

"Gabriel, I appreciate your coming here tonight. I realize how difficult it was for you."

Gabriel imagined a headline: PROFESSOR SLAIN WITH BROKEN BEER GLASS.

"I must ask you one more favour though, if you'll put up with me for another second."

Gabriel slipped his thumbs through his belt loops, held on tight.

"Would you tell me the names of your Métis grandparents? I would like to research your genealogy."

"My grandmother wasn't Métis for starters, she was a Blackfoot."

"I'll trace your grandfather for now — if you know his parents' names."

"If this is for my benefit, forget it. I don't want to know."

Phipps looked away, down at his slim white fingers wrapped tightly around the empty glass.

"No. It's for me. Morbid curiosity if you like."

Gabriel told Phipps the names and fled.

"I've got exciting news," said Dr. Phipps over the telephone.

Gabriel said what he could remember of the Hail Mary.

"You're forgetting something, aren't you?"

"Gabriel, I assure you, I had every intention of respecting your wish. If this news was less intriguing, I really would have kept it to myself."

"What is it?"

"Could you meet me?"

"Why not just tell me?"

"I've got it charted. It's easier to show you."

In the lounge, Gabriel drank beer until Phipps arrived. The professor was breathless and looked slightly deranged as he negotiated his path through the chairs. Trying to accommodate a cigarette, an overcoat and a briefcase, he looked apt to set himself or someone else on fire. He sat, caught the waitress's eye and ordered, all before sliding his briefcase onto the table and flipping the snaps. He could have been a magician about to produce rabbits. What he did draw out was a folder with two sheets inside that he slid around to face Gabriel. He pulled his chair over so he could see and point.

"So much more interesting than I dared hope. I went through all the standard texts, and the community histories. Then I took a short trip to Saskatchewan and checked some baptismal records. . . . "

"You drove to Saskatchewan for this?"

"Yes," said Phipps, as if there was nothing strange about having done so. "Anyway, I was finally able to determine what arm of the family your grandfather belonged to. It's a common enough name among the Métis which made it difficult but, as you can see here, I was able to place him. Your great grandmother's family is on this page. Right here."

Pyramids of names interconnected by lines, Gabriel's great-grandparents featured in red.

"Your grandfather's parents came straight to the Beaver Creek area of Alberta from Batoche. The timing must have been in the five years after the insurrection. I presume you are familiar with the story of Louis Riel and the Rebellion of 1885."

"You talked about it for two classes."

"That's *all* you know?"

"Why not? That's all anybody else in the class knew." The hurt question-mark face. Again, Gabriel relented. "Okay, I did hear my grandfather talk about Riel once or twice."

"Did he tell stories? He must have heard many as a child."

"Not that I recall. Just a line here and there. 'Don't bitch or they'll hang you like they did Riel.' Stuff like that."

"Did he mention Gabriel Dumont?"

"I only remember once. He was pissed off at this Ukrainian neighbour for shooting one of our dogs. It killed a sheep or something. And Baptiste told him — what was it? — that if Dumont had been chief of the Halfbreeds, the farmer would still be hoeing spuds in the Ukraine where he belonged. That's probably not right, but something like that."

"Sounds fascinating, your grandfather."

"Ya, you'd've been happier knowing him."

Phipps went back to his papers.

"Your great-grandparents were there in 1885. Batoche. I know that because, in one dispatch about the Battle of Fish Creek, your great-grandfather was mentioned. Dumont had fooled General Middleton's army into thinking the Métis force was much larger than it was. Moving from one place of cover to another, firing and moving on. Lighting brush fires. Imagine being fired at by who knows how many men from a wall of smoke. Worked on their nerves. That was the day Middleton had his hat shot off. So stiff-upper-lipped, he probably didn't realize he'd come within an inch of dying. If you think about it, all of Canadian history could have been different had that bullet been lower. Anyway, the Canadians had a few scouts and whatnot who knew the local Métis and one of them was sure he'd seen your great-grandfather running in the smoke."

"How much were the Halfbreeds outnumbered?"

"At Fish Creek? I don't know the actual numbers but I believe it was around five to one."

"They got shit-kicked in other words."

"Not at all. In fact Middleton withdrew from Tourond's Coulee convinced he was outnumbered and needed reinforcements. I do know the numbers involved in the final battle at Batoche. 850 Canadians against 300 Métis. It lasted most of four days. When the soldiers finally stormed Batoche, against orders, they took it easily. The Métis were down to firing nails and ball made out of melted kitchen utensils. One young soldier who ran down the hill broke into a house and found it empty except for a young girl laid out in her coffin. That girl had your great-grandmother's maiden name, though I can't otherwise verify a relationship.

"The reason your great-grandparents chose Beaver Creek as a place to go after Batoche has to do, I think, with two facts. Your great-grandfather was a rough carpenter and had worked with the Québécois carpenter who built the church and rectory at Batoche. The carpenter was married to a local Métis woman who I believe was your great-grandmother's sister, or at least her cousin. The carpenter's family moved to Beaver Creek around the time of the rebellion and it seems likely to me that your family followed them.

"If you look higher up, you'll see that the 'Batoche generation' of the two families was born of parents who came from Red River. There was a great exodus of Métis from Red River to the Saskatchewan area around 1869. The people who left were reacting to the atrocities and loss of power following the first seizure of power by Métis — Riel again — that year."

Phipps sat back. He was breathing hard as if he'd run a race.

"That's all I have right now but, if I went to Winnipeg, I'm sure I could track back even farther."

Phipps studied Gabriel and Gabriel could tell that once again he had disappointed his professor. He wasn't trying to look indifferent but he supposed indifference was what Phipps saw.

Phipps tried again, in a voice that retreated steadily.

"Your great-grandfather rode with Riel and Dumont. He must have known them personally. Your great-grandmother probably melted down all the metal in her cabin and poured it into casts to make bullets.

The whole family, possibly including your grandfather's older siblings, went with Red River carts to the Missouri Coteau for the last great buffalo hunts."

Gabriel got up to go. He offered his hand to Phipps for some reason.

"Thanks, Dr. Phipps. I'm not denying it's interesting."

Walking to his truck, Gabriel thought of something he might have added.

"It's interesting, but don't expect me to dig up my grandfather's pipe and smoke it."

13

In the summer after Gabriel's second year of university, he worked as a relief operator in a sour gas plant near Rocky Mountain House. It was one of the plants along the "Foothills Trend," a series of deep sour gas reservoirs in the east shadow of the Rockies. After the plants had cleaned the hydrogen sulphide out of the gas, it was pumped into a pipeline bound for California.

Inside the dial-lined control room, the hours were long. Baiting Gabriel was one way to pass them. He was studying for another class of steam ticket and they called him "professor," their last chance to give him shit before he, or the likes of him, came back in a position of authority over them. The situation, the social migration, often reminded Gabriel of Jeff Phipps and what it might be like to be him. Thinking about their last two meetings, Gabriel liked the way he'd been less and less, the reverse snobbery of it. On his first trip back to the city in early June, he phoned Phipps and invited him for a beer.

The summer Phipps had a different look than the winter one. The suit and tie were gone, replaced by an anti-nukes T-shirt and shorts; a skinny set of amazingly hairy legs between the canvas bottom of the shorts and his knee-high sports socks. He was more relaxed and even made a joke to begin about what had gone before, something about the gas plant and that, if Gabriel had to assimilate, he'd at least chosen a lucrative career to assimilate into. Gabriel replied with the line he'd once held back from Phoebe.

"Not much call for buffalo hunters these days."

Phipps appreciated the joke and, first hurdle leapt, they moved on to other things.

Gabriel asked a question that had been forming in his mind all the way along the highway that day: wasn't Phipps in the wrong faculty? He seemed, on the surface, to like history better than literature. Sudden gloom told him he'd gone straight to another area of pain.

"I don't know what to say to that."

"You don't have to say anything."

"No, I mean, it's quite perceptive of you. It's something I've certainly dithered over a great deal." Phipps looked both ways and then confessed. "You see, I'm a poet. Or I'd like to be. I don't know when you actually become one."

"You say it like it's a sin."

"It's because I'm an English professor. Half of us have a secret stash of poems, short stories, novels. To come out of the closet and proclaim yourself a writer — to the other professors, I mean — is to set yourself up as a rival to the whole tradition of literature. A student can apprentice, and then give it up if it doesn't suit him. But, unless I was to instantly publish, and to great critical acclaim, I could easily look a fool."

"Do you care?"

"Yes."

"So you're still in the closet."

"Yes."

Gabriel understood that he'd been trusted with a confidence. He let the topic move on.

Later, when a quantity of drink had been taken, Phipps said, "I don't want to sound maudlin, but I was very glad when you called."

"I was a prick the last two times."

Phipps didn't deny it. "And I was prying."

The next time into town, it felt imperative that Gabriel call Phipps again. He had enjoyed their beer together. If he let it be the last one, Phipps could easily believe that Gabriel was only fixing things with his conscience, that the meeting amounted to nothing more.

Gabriel had drinking plans with Clive that night. Once they were settled in the bar, he went to the phone, found Phipps in, and invited him down.

Sitting with Clive, waiting for Phipps to arrive, Gabriel began to worry about the mixture of human compounds he had just contrived to concoct. Cynic meets enthusiast. Professional student meets professor. Gabriel could think of dozens of ways the potion might fizzle or explode.

But he hadn't entirely known his ingredients. Within seconds of Phipps's entrance, the introduction and exchange of titles, Phipps was laughing, laughing so hard he had occasion to frequently demist his glasses on the pulled tail of his T-shirt. Enjoying a better reaction than he was used to from Gabriel, Clive found new heights — or depths. He busily unpeeled himself, revealing ever shabbier motives all the way down to the bone.

The tradition of a summer was established that night. It continued, enjoyably.

> CLIVE: Phippsy, I think you should get a tubal ligation.
>
> PHIPPS: (Ha, ha) That's generally done to women, idiot, in that fallopian tubes are required.
>
> CLIVE: Then tie a knot in whatever you have.

PHIPPS: Why would this be such a great service to me?

CLIVE: That's funny. You get the point then.

PHIPPS: No, frankly. I don't.

CLIVE: More service to you. We'd advertise you as 100% safe and, when the women gather, Gabriel and I would slip in like whippets and share in the spoils.

PHIPPS: (Ha, ha) Brilliant, Clive. Up to your usual standard. I guess you think the world would lose less if I were sterilized than if the job were done on either of you.

CLIVE: Gabriel, give us the Halfbreed viewpoint on this.

GABRIEL: I'd sterilize both of you, if you aren't already. Not that it would improve your sex lives.

CLIVE: Well, I can't believe it, personally. Here I am chumming around with a proven aborigine and a PhD from McGill and neither of you have brought one woman into my life.

PHIPPS: (Ha, ha) The Métis are not aboriginal, and my PhD was from Queen's. My undergrad was done at McGill.

CLIVE: Okay, okay. Points well taken. But I think we need signs around our necks. "Intellectually Stimulating Professor of English Literature," "Sexually Vigorous Halfbreed."

PHIPPS: How about yours, Clive?

GABRIEL: "Sexually Deficient Civil Servant."

CLIVE: No, no. I'd be content with "Friend of the Above."

PHIPPS: (Ha, ha) That's good. In James Joyce's days in Dublin, he cited his occupation as friend of a medical student. He shared digs in a Martello tower in Dun Laoghaire with Oliver St. James Gogarty who was a medical student, you see. Gogarty was the Buck Mulligan character in ULYSSES....

CLIVE: (IN THE VOICE OF A RACE ANNOUNCER) And he's off! At the first turn it's Stifling Boredom running neck-and-neck with Fearsome Pedant.

GABRIEL: Don't be so inconsiderate, Phipps. You know how Clive hates the idea that he might learn something.

CLIVE: I do not. Go ahead, Gabriel. Tell me something you know. Tell me how you get gasoline from a tar ball. Or, better yet, tell me the significance of colour in cow turds.

PHIPPS: (Ha, ha)

When Phipps first suggested the trip to Batoche, that was treated as a joke too, though he certainly didn't mean it as one. Phipps still had it percolating in his mind that, if Gabriel were to go to the scene of the 1885 Métis Rebellion, something would happen, something marvelously kinetic.

CLIVE: I'll bet you're right, Phipps. Gabriel beating his way through the brush. Is there a river there?

PHIPPS: Your stout grasp of history and geography amazes me once again, Clive. Yes, there is a river, the South Saskatchewan by name.

CLIVE: By the river. Bushes by the river. Gripped suddenly by ancestral knowledge, he puts his ear to a horse bun and detects the sound of footsteps, even though the approaching feet are in moccasins. He sits in the trail, in more horse buns, and a beautiful Métis princess, Running Naked, appears from around the bend....

GABRIEL: Forget it, Phipps. Why should I live out your fantasies for you? I don't want to go there.

CLIVE: It's an old professorial habit, Gabriel. Phipps would feel like he was slumming if he actually *did* anything. Far better to have someone's sputum and tobacco-stained diary.

But before the summer's end, Clive had bought into the idea. As an adventure. He bought into it literally in the sense that he purchased a new yellow straw cowboy hat to wear on the trip, a highly symbolic act for someone who seldom bought retail. It was the wrong kind, Gabriel was quick to inform him; the brim was almost flat and it had a string and wooden bead under the chin like a child's. But Clive apparently wanted it like that. After the purchase, he would talk of little else but the trip.

Fine, said Gabriel, the two of you go. Clive insisted that this would not do. Deficient as he was, they needed Gabriel — as their touchstone, their passport, their legitimacy. Clive didn't like going anywhere that he didn't have an "in".

So Gabriel consented, with conditions. He would make no acquaintances on this trip. If his family were mentioned, he would stoutly deny everything, claiming to be an exchange student from the Sudan.

The second Friday in August, the wheels of Phipps's untrustworthy American compact hit the highway, the swarming Trans-Canada east of Calgary. Phipps coughed more than usual, seemed intimidated by having so many cars moving toward him. He leaned the wheel a bit right, to counteract either an alignment problem or a compulsion to suicide. Everyone was relieved when he turned off onto Highway 9, narrower and almost empty.

In the bucket seat beside Phipps, Clive sat wearing his hat, held on against the strong breeze from the window by the string, the wooden bead cinched tight to his underchin. He smoked and wagged a Havana cigar and its smoke and sparks flew back to Gabriel, who blunted the larger coals landing on the plastic seat with his removed boot.

On the highway to Drumheller, bending over and around glacial undulations, a case of beer was cracked. The drinking was brisk and the case was so close to gone as they dove into the dinosaur graveyard at Drumheller that it was necessary to stop in a lazy morning hotel tavern for more drinking and the purchase of a fresh, dripping case for the road.

Surfacing beyond the Red Deer River, the land beneath them continued to roll, the waves slightly gentler. The morning cool cooked off in the straight-above sunshine and their sweating backs stuck through T-shirts to the plastic. Every squirm, produced an adhesive rip. The Saskatchewan border neared, was passed. The only wildlife encountered since Calgary: two dead gophers and one greased rattlesnake — and one other carload of early day drunks. Stranded between outhouses, these four stood on the shoulder of the road, pissing without cover or embarrassment.

Then, beyond Kindersley, as if the carpet of land had been given a jerk, the earth flattened beneath them. Land-dwarfed toy, a tiny piece on God's great chessboard, the car hugged to a strip of grey infinitely long.

In Saskatoon, Clive demanded a pilgrimage to the Right Honourable John G. Diefenbaker Centre at the University of Saskatchewan. The man who brought the Conservative Party (Clive's current party) back to power in 1957; the man who made the nation forget the party's disgrace during the Depression. The stigma left on the party by one Westerner erased by another Westerner. Clive led the way humbly through this shrine, paying particular attention to objects Dief the Chief had handled in life, as if his presence were most concentrated there. Gabriel had never seen his friend so close to being reverent. It was in hopes of deflating that reverence that he reached and took a Diefenbaker hat off a John A. Macdonald hat rack and put it on Clive's head. Alarms went off. A guard came and, in the world-weariest way, replaced the hat and scolded them. Pressed, he admitted that it happened almost every day, but was usually done by children.

Before leaving town, another case of beer was bought for the stretch run to Batoche. Feeling his goal near, Phipps refused beer and bought coffee, drinking it through a rip in the plastic top even as he complained of a burned tongue. He nailed the accelerator to the floor. The car vibrated under them. They had to be in Batoche by sundown. And they were. Long enough in light to examine the outside of the church and its rectory.

The white steeple of the church was like a pair of very slim and delicate hands pointed in prayer. The rectory sported bullet holes almost a century old. Gabriel's great grandfather helped build these buildings, Phipps said grandly. Pointing at the bullet marks: the army fired on the church and rectory even though only priests and nuns were inside. The Canadians thought the clergy were siding with the Métis; the Métis thought the clergy had betrayed them to the Canadians.

That was an interesting one, said Clive. Push the button again.

They followed Phipps across a grassy swale to the graveyard, and between the ranks of dead to the far end where the fence marked the cliff's edge above the river's broad meander. Gabriel Dumont's bulky scalloped stone stood there in its place of honour. Phipps read the plaque aloud, his voice quivering a bit with the intensity of his feelings. The river had turned to gold. I have a hunch, he said, that Gabriel was named for this man. Not Gabe Kaplan? said Clive. And Phipps did not laugh, not smile. Everyone was to shut up here, he was as much as telling them. OK, Phippsy, said Clive and walked away.

Gabriel also moved away. Walked the rows alone, looking back from time to time at the unmoving professor. A small silhouette, dwarfed by the stone and the giant sky of blue-gold. Gabriel couldn't help but wonder what a burly, shaggy buffalo hunter would think if he looked out of that rock and saw Phipps. Gabriel scanned the sticks and stones, saw a few name plates marked with his great-grandmother's maiden name, his grandfather's surname. Etched, scratched. Phipps bowed to Dumont's stone and came to join him, finding from the well-thumbed sheets of family tree in his pocket a couple of dead he was certain were Gabriel's kin. Gabriel felt mostly depressed by this. One of his people, somebody a little like his mother, beneath crooked, weathered wood; the nail to the crosspiece, a few delicate welts of rust showing through the time-demolished edge.

On special occasions, after mass, said Phipps, the local people march in procession to the graveyard for benediction. In a couple of years it would be the centennial of the last Métis rebellion and big events were planned for this spot. It was Jeff Phipps's wish to attend.

Don't tell anyone, but he was planning an epic poem which he hoped to read on that day.

Joining them, Clive said, you really know how to throw a party, Phippsy. Gabriel said, let's find a bar.

They established themselves in the tavern of a hotel in the nearby town of Duck Lake. A bulbous juke box gave out an unrelieved stream of rock tunes at high volume. The pool table was busy, each player knowing exactly where on its side to belt it so no balls hung up when it shucked in coins. But the tavern had more empty tables than full and a corner fenced out by logs for dancing stayed dark and empty. Seeing the way they gawked around, the bartender/waiter told them, by way of apology, that tonight was bingo night and he doubted they'd see much of a crowd.

Phipps, Clive and Gabriel nurtured an awkward silence for some time, not sure suddenly how to act beyond the ritual hoisting and pouring down of beer. When conversation did begin it was about the tents and sleeping bags crushed into the trunk of Phipps's car. The hard ground did not beckon either Clive or Gabriel when made-up beds of some sort were available just a flight of stairs away. Clive imagined himself whaling away at plastic pegs and felt certain his rock would strike and blacken his thumb. Gabriel predicted that a couple would erect a tent close to theirs and would make loud love all night. There was also the matter that none of them had seen a campground of any kind. Phipps, arguing for a night of cold purity under the stars, was overruled.

Phipps lost this argument but he did not wilt. He took firm possession of tomorrow. Tomorrow they would see the rifle pits the Métis used to baffle the Canadian army that so outnumbered them.

"850 to 300," said Gabriel, remembering his lessons.

Phipps would do his best to pinpoint the place where Batoche's ferry cables were lowered on Dumont's orders to snare the heavily armed paddle wheeler "Northcote." Dumont hoped to capture the whole boat and pick off its soldiers from the cover of the wooded bank but a screw-up in communication resulted in the command coming a fraction late. The cable ripped off the smokestacks, started a fire. But the boat and its soldiers got away downstream.

They would return to the bridge by which they had crossed the South Saskatchewan this evening. It marked the approximate location of Gabriel Dumont's home and competing ferry business. They would search the area for any remains of the house's foundations. They would think upon the ransack, robbery and burning of that house, the fact that the army bore away from it, amazingly, a billiards table. They would note the narrow river lots (an inheritance from New France) into which much of the land was still divided.

With an air of resignation, Clive ordered a fresh jug of beer. Like the juke box so well stocked with quarters, Phipps could not be stopped unless his personal power source failed.

Had they noticed the decorations on the walls, Phipps asked? Gabriel Dumont and Louis Riel were featured, oil on board likenesses based on familiar photos of the two. The beverage room was in fact dedicated to Louis Riel and the clientele, save for themselves (he caught himself and said, save for Clive and himself) were exclusively Native. Had they noticed this? Clive said that some such piece of sensory data had poked its way through to register on his brain. Phipps then launched himself into a vigorous account of the Battle of Duck Lake, fought near this location in the year of 1885.

Another Métis victory. Over the Mounties this time. Riel present and wandering around in the cross fire waving a crucifix. Dumont led the troops, took a bullet across the skull. He is said to have raved murderously at the prisoners taken by the Métis side, but was still able to sit a horse in the glorious return to Batoche. Phipps had met a woman at an academic gathering who was distantly related to Dumont. Once, when she was a little girl, her family had been paid a visit by the old hunt chieftain. She and her siblings had crawled back out after their bedtime and, peering down through a railing, she had seen the top of Gabriel Dumont's head. Through the thinning white of his hair, she saw the scar the bullet had left, inflamed by the night's imbibing.

Gabriel and Clive, more deeply into their beer by now, looked out of their blue halo of smoke for signs of this history. Dumont hugged his rifle and glowered at them off his wall. Riel looked over their heads, probably into some mystic plane no one else could see. The crowd of the living got on with their pool and their conversations and their romances and their drinking, in a peaceful, detached way that bore no obvious sign or scar of history's dealings with their ancestors.

Clive did not ordinarily drink to excess. A cagey drinker, he would nurse one drink all night while giving the impression of having consumed many. Tonight, Gabriel noticed that his friend was not holding back and had begun to pivot in his chair, his upper body rotating on the ball of his spine. He drew the wooden bead beneath his chin up and down in approximate syncopation. Controlling his lips and tongue carefully against unseen forces, he told Gabriel and Phipps that his state paid them the highest compliment. That he was now so obviously shit-faced expressed the great trust he felt for them, the great safety he felt in their company. And now, if they would excuse him, he would like to go upstairs and throw up.

Soon after Clive's departure, the bartender/waiter came round and announced to all that it was time to drink up and go home. Phipps and Gabriel discussed the merits of buying a case from off-sales. They decided that, with the heat and all, it wasn't so much an option as a necessity.

Each narrow step of stairs let out a wail when a foot touched. Phipps tilted into the railing and it yawed and cracked, and very nearly broke off under him. They found their narrow rooms. In Gabriel's, a fly spun on the floor. The smell of smoke was stifling in the heat. Taking two beers each, they went to the end of the hall where the door under the blurry red exit sign had been propped open with a laceless black running shoe. On an outside landing at the head of the fire escape, they sat together and dangled their legs.

Two pick-up trucks remained in the parking lot below. They had been pulled around so they faced in opposite directions, the driver's side cab windows as close as their rearview mirrors allowed. The driver who faced their way leaned over. The sharp rip of a beer case opening. He handed a bottle across the gap to the driver in the other truck. The reaching arms connecting at the bottle gave Gabriel a comical image of conjugation. Truck fuck, he said to Phipps.

But Phipps was off in a weightier thought, more substantial symbolism. Trucks and tractor cabs were the true homes of these men, he said. He bet they felt more at home with the greasy rags and the tangles of wire and tools on the floor, the butt-flooded ashtrays, than they did in the cozy tidiness enforced by wives on their houses. Phipps saw rugged individuality and territorial imperative in the way these two trucks were parked. In what he called "this closely shared moment," neither man would leave his truck and sit in the cab of the other.

Then, reversing his field, Phipps cursed himself bitterly for being the kind of person who has to intellectualize everything. He was utterly incapable of sitting quietly, like Gabriel, enjoying a cold beer, listening to a distant chorus of frogs, appreciating the moment for what the moment, in its simplest terms, was. Oh Christ, there I go again....

The attack became more brutal. That's why I drink and smoke so much, he charged. Because I'm too busy thinking and explaining everything to pay attention. Whenever I finish a beer or a smoke, I don't remember it, I don't remember getting any pleasure from it, so I have another.

Bad news, thought Gabriel. Without Clive, Phipps's mood was in a tailspin. Only a matter of time until the gloom got round to Gabriel.

It soon did: Phipps begging Gabriel to feel something about the place they were now in, about the stories he'd been spinning in the bar all night. Open yourself, let it pour in. Pour in another ounce of anything, said Gabriel, and it may return swiftly. In a drunk and dreary way, Gabriel told Phipps again that it was not this Gabriel who had ridden with Dumont, prayed with Riel; it was some long dead member of a scattered family. For all anyone knew, the fellow may not have had a heroic hair or bone. He may have spent the whole seige of Batoche under his bed whimpering that he'd like to kill Riel for bringing them to this hopelessly outnumbered end.

Phipps put his elbows up on the rough slivered rail. He pressed the sweating beer bottle to his forehead with both hands. The bottle slipped, shot off the lubricated slope, and exploded among the rocks in the gravel pad below.

"Well, I'd love it," he said.

"Love what?"

"To be a Métis. I'd dress funny. I'd sing old songs in French. I'd be here for the anniversary of the Insurrection every year. I'd love it."

"Come on, Phipps. Let's call it a night."

14

Morning in Duck Lake brought terrible hangovers. Aspirins were shared out from a tiny tin over breakfast. A waitress in the cafe down the street slopped their coffee cups full and they lowered the stuff into queasy stomachs. Phipps's suggestions that they should get going were barely a whimper and nothing happened until noon.

Then, as the townspeople wandered in for lunch, Clive reared back in his chair. Dementia in red-veined eyes, he cried, "Hair of the dog!"

In the front passenger seat of the car, Clive cuddled the ten remaining beer. Phipps drove as if the gently curving road had become, for him, a gravel-backed python, sudden changes in shape demanding hair trigger reactions on the steering wheel. Gabriel sat in the back trying to tie a leader to a fishing line.

Just before they reached the river, Gabriel called for a right turn down a steep, overhung trail. Phipps worried the car along it, at pains to stay astraddle the grass-exploded middle. They held their ears against the squeal of branch on paint and glass.

At the bottom, in a wide spot by the river, Phipps and Clive stayed behind Gabriel in the walk to the river's edge, respectful and subdued, almost cowering, as Gabriel flourished his fishing rod and announced that they would never catch a fish at this location in a million years.

After the strong green river had shoved his hook ashore a few times, Gabriel reeled the line back and tied the hook to the rod. He joined Clive and Phipps, supine in the shade of aspens, and grabbed a beer from the case beside them. The warm froth exploded in his mouth and he cursed them for a pair of eggheads. "A river a long spit away and you don't put the beer in to cool."

He made a corral of rocks and Clive, squatting beside, hugged the case and worried aloud that they would be carried away in the current.

"What do you care? You like getting sick or what?"

Clive held his bottle in the air and spoke to it.

"This is the world's most magical fluid. What else in man's vast arsenal of medicines can half kill you at night and restore you to health in the morning?"

Phipps laughed from under his tree and Gabriel took it as a sign that the crisis in him had passed.

Gabriel had no sooner stretched out on the uneven ground than Phipps began asking, cajoling and finally begging him to return to the river to fish.

"Phipps, there isn't a fish living can stay put in that current."

"It's not the fish," Phipps endeavoured to explain, "it's the image.

You performing an age-old rite. The sun in my eyes turns you into a silhouette. Very primeval. Jungian almost."

Gabriel reached for his fishing rod. "This is an expensive, modern fibreglass rod, Phipps. Attached to it here is an expensive reel that allows you to free line with the touch of a thumb." He twanged the line. "Invisible in water, Phipps, strong enough to land a ten-pound fighting trout."

Phipps ignored him, stared off into some nonexistent place.

"Primeval man. The hunter, black against the sky. Cast for me, Gabriel. Just cast."

Clive had tipped his hat back and was watching Phipps closely.

"You know, Phippsy," he said after a while, "sometimes you sound queer."

Far from insulted, Phipps seemed glad the subject had been raised.

"Actually, Clive, I wonder if you're not right. Last night, I had what I think was a queer insight. I was standing at the urinal — pissing..."

"Thanks for the clarification."

"... and I realized that the configuration of holes at the bottom of the urinal was the exact shape of an erect penis pointing at me. Well, maybe not the exact shape, more of a phallic design: two parallel rows of holes and they connect at the front to a circle."

"Shit," said Clive, "he is queer. Not that I'm prejudiced."

"I don't know. I mean I should know by now, shouldn't I? But possibly the right opportunity has never presented itself. It would certainly explain my failure with women."

When the time came to think about food and the next night's lodgings, a fresh argument developed. Phipps was still keen on a camping experience, either that or a return to Duck Lake. Clive and Gabriel were having none of either. Clive wanted a TV in his room. "A TV is an essential part of the hotel experience." Gabriel wanted a double bed and a table beside it with a lamp on top by which he could read his day-old newspaper. Clive wanted a Caesar salad with his dinner. Gabriel wanted to shower in a tub containing no one else's hairs but his own. Phipps's charge of bourgeois materialism and a serious lack in their spirits of adventure did nothing to alter their plans.

In the new town, the new hotel, the new tavern, the atmosphere was surely different. Lighted American beer signs and plastic coats of arms were the featured motifs in the beverage room. The table they took was one of the last available in the spacious and well-lit beer parlour. It was a white town and the Saturday night crowd was mostly white as well. Whites were sitting mostly with whites, Natives with Natives.

There were more women present than there had been the night

before and Clive thought that this and the racial assortment improved their chances of seeing some "local colour." He meant arguments and fights, "the small town forms of rut." At that moment, action around the pool table was promising to fulfil his hopes without delay. A tall, spare and well-oiled fellow wearing the winter liner from a welding helmet was in a clumsy rage over quarters and whose turn it was to play. He was sure he had placed quarters in the coin slot to reserve the right to play the winner of the last match. Now, the quarters were gone, into the machine, and some other pair was racking the eight balls and chalking up.

"What a fucking asshole," said a member of the team about to play.

"You stole my fucking quarters!" screamed the tall man from under his tightly clinging felt headgear.

But the manager of the bar intervened and the two near-combatants were soon hugging each other around the necks while mouthing parting statements of affection.

"I still say you're an asshole."

"You're just a low-down quarter thief."

Gabriel didn't share Clive's enthusiasm for seeing any of this local colour. The previous day's drinking had left him feeling brittle and hunted. If there was a flare-up here, he had a strong premonition they would be among the first burned. For that matter, they could be spark, kindling and wood in a handy three-pack; and finally, the ashes everyone hauled, with the locals pissing on them to see if they were out.

Gabriel looked at Clive and Phipps. Not a reassuring sight. One, refusing to take off his toy cowboy hat, playing away with the wooden bead on its string, looking for all the world like a pansy, or at least a small town person's idea of what a pansy looks like; and the other, Phipps, busily appraising every man who pushed through the door. Gabriel remembered the bars back home, and the many bars he'd been in along the trail of rigs and gas plants. In all those bars, and in all those long hours of pouring down draft, he'd never felt quite as vulnerable as he did now. How pleasant it would be to be at some other table, in some other (any other) pair of boots or shit-kickers. From that vantage, a person could enjoy the view of the oddballs at this table. You could joke about them all night, if there was nothing else to talk about; and, if things got really slow, you could even beat their heads in. It was always best to take out your frustrations on strangers — the stranger the better.

Two men and a woman appeared among the musical instruments on the low dais behind the dance floor. They wore tight-fitting cowboy clothes that glittered, lemon yellow scarves knotted round their throats. They were doing the things that musicians do before they play: cuffing out-of-tune chords, wrenching tuning pegs, rolling thunder across the drums and capping it off with a cymbal clash. Amongst the feedback squeals, they called, "Testing, testing;" and once, from the woman, the words "this fucking thang" before she realized that this fucking thang really was working after all.

Ten minutes or so of this and they finally bellied up to their microphones in a more meaningful way and unleashed a blast of country and western into the room. For half a song, the crowd was too stunned to move. Then a chunky woman, a dance floor pioneer from away back, wearing an untucked blouse and a flammable looking pair of orange pants, tip-toed between the tables to the parquet floor. She was alone there for a minute and she did a sort of miniature ballet, involving only those parts of herself below the knee. This was to put in time while her partner was coming forward.

The man she awaited was a near giant. Lumbering along the same path she had taken, he looked unaccustomed to walking. He teetered from side to side and the heels of his cowboy boots were worn away on the outsides from the pressure exerted by his bow legs. His hair was short and flat except for a bit that spiked up in back, obedient to the air vent in the John Deere cap he'd left dangling on the post of his chair.

Reaching the dance floor, he took the chunky woman in his arms with great delicacy. They moved very smoothly; someone could have been pulling them around on a wheeled cart.

Into Gabriel's ear, Clive shouted, "I want a woman!" From the other side, Phipps yelled, "Does the male singer strike you as attractive?" All seemed, in that moment, lost.

But, as the musicians got more deeply into the song, and as more dancers flung themselves into the mob on the floor, Gabriel had another thought: despite all the signs of danger, a momentum existed here, a pure stream pouring. To stem the current for whatever reason, even survival, would be both rude and cowardly. Better to commit himself. Damn the rocks and deadheads!

Accepting this, he took the measure of the country and western song and began tossing in lines of his own for the benefit of Clive and Phipps.

> *He was a smooth talking trucker*

"A dismal motherfucker"

> *Always disappearing*
> *up or down some endless grade.*

> *In every truck stop cafe*
> *Another waitress loved him*
> *Loved him even though she knew*

"He was queer as Jeffery Phipps."

"That doesn't even rhyme, Gabriel. Besides I'm not certain yet."

Then it was happening; a piece out of one of the scenarios Gabriel had imagined in his paranoia for this evening. On the far side of the room, a man had boarded his legs in a way that made them look wooden. (Anyone considering the farming life should have a long look at how many are stoved-up and short of arms, legs and fingers.) He was heading for them, even though their table was not on the way to any exit or place to piss. The man's shoulders seemed too wide, his chest too deep for the rest of him. He could have been dropped out of an airplane as a child. A dark green workshirt encased him and was mottled by black patches (grease). The fingers jutting out of his too-long sleeves were all there, but were thick and brown like packs of smokies. Beer bellied, swarthy — his eyebrows met over his broad, flat nose.

He kept coming and, when he got to them, he grabbed a chair from another table, twirled it on one leg and sat astride. He looked over one, then another, then the other of them without saying a word. Finally he said, "This an asshole convention or can anyone join?"

Gabriel's grip tightened around his beer glass.

The intruder took another long look at them from under his mat of eyebrow. He let out a wheezy laugh then offered his hand for shaking.

"My name's Frank."

The other two introduced themselves eagerly and then it was Gabriel's turn. Hanging on to Gabriel's hand longer than was necessary, Frank squinted and squeezed his lips together so they rolled up inside-out, showing wet and pink.

"Gabriel who?" He held on still, implying that if Gabriel wanted his hand back, he'd better answer. Lie, thought Gabriel, but didn't.

"You from here then?" For a second, Frank gripped the hand even harder. "Familiar name in these parts."

"No."

"You look like you should be." But the grip relaxed.

Into the conversation, Phipps came barging. He told Frank that Gabriel probably did have relatives "in these parts."

"Guess that makes you a Halfbreed," said Frank.

Gabriel examined the situation with scientific detachment. He measured the distance from Frank to himself. The fat part of the table separated them. He glanced behind, negotiating the fairly short and clear path to the nearest door. Getting Phipps out would be like herding pigs but Clive would know how to use his legs if there were trouble.

"That's what it makes me."

Phipps intruded again. "Are you Métis as well, Frank?"

"Métis? What's that?"

"Halfbreed," said Gabriel, with a smile for Phipps. Another wheezy laugh, this one touching off a coughing fit. Frank recovered, balanced a ball of spit on his tongue, poised to let fly. Not seeing a receptacle or else having an attack of manners, he swallowed it.

"Hell no. I'm no Halfbreed. I'm a Uke."

"A Ukrainian?"

"That's what I just said." To Gabriel: "Your friend here deaf?" He pronounced it "deef" as in Diefenbaker.

"No, but he's smart as a post."

Frank started to laugh again but Gabriel told him to hold on. He didn't want to see anyone cough himself to death at their table. This struck Clive and Phipps as exceptionally rude and Gabriel could tell they were just now beginning to worry of danger. This was funny in that Gabriel's fears had evaporated. He recognized Frank now and felt silly that he hadn't recognized him sooner. In a less shakey mood he would have been able to tell as soon as the man stood up. Gabriel had met Frank often in places like this, mainly because Frank always felt compelled to meet him. Every unmet person is a challenge to Frank. He must come over and find out who you are and if you're all right. He's not a fighter. He may cause fights from time to time by finding out that someone isn't all right, but he doesn't participate. In fact, once he's started a fight, Frank always tries to stop it. If he can stop a fight before anyone is hurt, he feels good for a week. Frank was probably well liked in this room, and the three of them were safe in his company. They might even have some fun.

The false alarm in Clive and Phipps mounted to strumming pitch as Frank launched into his opinion of Halfbreeds.

"There's plenty of Breeds here alright. Even though a bunch of them got run off over at Batoche a long time ago. Shot up and run off. I think that was in the '20s. No, couldn't have been. My Old Man came from the Old Country in '18 and the Batoche thing was long over then. I guess the few Breeds that stuck around must have bred like rabbits since. Maybe that's why we call them Breeds." A thick stubby finger pointing around the room. "Joe there's a Breed. And Alphonse. Antoine. Then there's all the Indians. Lots of Indians here too. Alright guys, Indians, but you gotta watch them when they're drunk. Turn on ya. As for the Breeds, I get along with most of them. Alphonse cheats at cards, though."

Phipps kept raising his finger, opening his mouth. Looking for a gap to charge through. Finally:

"The Rebellion was in 1885, and the Métis were hardly run off. Some took land scrip and stayed here; others preferred to turn their backs on a place that meant unfairness and atrocity to them. They moved beyond the survey to the north and west."

Gabriel explained to Frank that Jeffery was a professor.

"Ah," said Frank, all being explained. "Buy you a beer?"

Despite the anaemic efforts of a wall-mounted air conditioner, heat pulsed out of the roomful of living bodies and lay trapped. Dancers returned from polkas and jives streaming sweat, their armpits and backs soaked through. A ripe smell took command.

Curiosity about Frank's latest find brought tables swinging in to abut their own and Gabriel catalogued the incoming parade. Cross-legged women, kicking and smoking, like a seated chorus line. Men who leaned their elbows on the table and hung their heads in the cradle of hunched shoulders. Men who sat back so far they were barely part of the group (which was the point), hands in their pockets, chins on their chests, maybe a shiny boot sole leaning against the table's edge. Women who held onto their men's arms and whispered things that didn't seem to register. An Indian man, in long braids and a black felt hat punched out into a bowl; around the hat's circumference, a plaster of feathers that reminded Gabriel of what might happen if you were riding a motorcycle at high speed and hit a chicken. Men with their sleeves rolled up, Popeye forearms so white above brown hands they looked like risen and hair-sprouted bread dough. On many of the soft, hairless undersides of these arms, Gabriel saw what he and his friends used to call "the milking muscle." The Indian and Halfbreed arms were mostly slim and sinewed, and usually gouged with purple scars.

Phipps, separated from Gabriel and Clive by the influx of people and tables, was in a state of near constant outrage. The cardplayer Alphonse had taken up a chair beside Phipps, and Gabriel had seen at first how this filled Phipps's face with enthusiasm. The search for original colloquial anecdote could really get rolling now. But Alphonse cheated at more than cards. Through the music and the solid roar of voices, Gabriel caught chips of the conversation between them:

". . . an asshole, that Riel. . . "
". . . only true Western Canadian patriot. . . !"
". . . crazier than a shithouse rat. . . "
". . . Eastern Establishment view transposed. . . !"

"... Dumont knew he was off his..."
"... their spiritual relationship..."
"... barely sit a horse..."

In his place at the table, Clive had begun again to rotate. He bravely rode the crest of a wave of liquor that would probably bear him to the lip of a toilet again tonight. His eyeballs were a blur, the anaesthetized pupil shrunken and unmoving. As Gabriel watched, the too-flat brim of the cowboy hat tilted toward the ceiling. A coyote moan of pure horniness:

"I need a woman!"

Heads turned toward Clive with a certain interest, but not many of them women. The chunky woman who had been first to the dance floor did look and she said, "You can have a dance with me if you like. But you keep your hands to yourself."

And so the night proceeded.

A would-be future Prime Minister of Canada cavorting on the parquet floor — how? — like a newborn calf; the first happy awkward leaps upon discovering that the world contains milk. The chunky woman good-naturedly adapting.

And Phipps:

"... Native self-government..."
"... pay enough taxes already..."
"... man the barricades...!"
"... ain't that much good wood left round these parts..."
"... need another charismatic leader...!"
"... need five bucks myself. How are you fixed?"

Gabriel sat at the heart of the noise and the cluttered tavern air and he knew at last where he was. This was the museum of small town bar life. Pay your buck and Gabriel will take you on a tour. Left alone by armies, this and a thousand other towns were dying so slowly they didn't even know it, the carcass slowly picked by an outflux of youth. Unblessed by economic opportunity meant blessed by a chance to stay the same, albeit with a hole where the people Gabriel's age should have been.

And where were the young men Gabriel's age tonight? Playing poker in a camp, watching a dirty video, working graveyard shift on a rig? Maybe they were in the city, at a party full of city people; the country mice trying to fit in, but betrayed by the square asses they'd shoved into pairs of designer blue jeans.

Worse yet, some might have found their way into bars full of people who also didn't fit in anywhere in particular. If an argument started, they might find out, quickly but too late, that misfittedness isn't a good glue after all — when a certain lack of rules about things like broken beer bottles and knives became evident.

But this place, tonight, was safe as a swim in a slow river. Gabriel sat back in a pool of it, and enjoyed with a quiet mind. He let the conversation flow over him and through.

When would they have quota again? When would it be worth more to raise a calf than to knock it on the head at birth? Stockers and feeders, canners and cutters. And as for pigs I won't have the rootin' sonsabitches on my place. Hockey season long over and about to begin again. Oilers might bring the Stanley Cup to Western Canada for the first time. And who gives a fuck if they do (pardon my French)? If Saskatoon ain't good enough to be an NHL town, they can all kiss my ass, I won't watch the damn thing. They play like fairies nowadays anyway. Fairies and professional wrestlers. One farmer had trouble with losing wrenches. Another advised: when you get a new wrench hit it on the floor four-five times. Break its legs so it can't run away. Forecasts of a new Great Depression. A Depression to end all Depressions. Dire patterns seen in the way the rains had not come. The sucking quality of wind. A reliable ancient Indian from Cutknife says there will be a drought next summer and that the winter before it will be cold enough to freeze the balls off a brass monkey. The spleen of someone else's recently butchered pig contradicts the Indian and all agree that they will have to wait to see how the muskrats build their houses to know for sure. And what about those Russians fucking (pardon me) around with the jet stream? Bending arctic air over the prairies on its way to freeze the Florida orange crop.

The way out of all this mess? Shoot your herd. Sell out to the Hutterites and then go to work selling them farm machinery. Drink yourself to death is a popular suggestion, it being seen from afar as more fun.

Or separate. If you think you'll ever get a fair shake in Canada you're crazier than I thought. Yessir, separate. The Royal Mounted Farmer's Cooperative of Saskatchewan. When the choice is an eastern housewife or a western farmer, who do you think's going to win? Wind up holding the short end of the stick every time. The shit end of the stick. In the shit, in the grease, and in the soup. But if we separate, who are we going to trust? The oil companies? The flip and fly real estate bastards? The foreclosing fuckers (excuse me) of banks?

Aw the hell with it. The hell with them all. What's it matter in the long run anyway? I'll be long dead before.... They'll blow us to rat shit first. Turn us into so many rice crispies. Might as well get pissed, right after bending over and kissing your ass goodbye. Put your money in beer and at least you get to see it one more time, briefly, before she flushes away forever. Bring back capital punishment. Bring back John Diefenbaker. Disband the Mounties. My mother saves string, by the way, and I think she's right to. Never know when it'll come in handy.

When all is said and done, the bowlegged giant, his arm tucked round the chunky woman, wants to buy Clive's hat and Clive, seeing the main chance, puts it up for bid. He gets an offer of twenty-five dollars and takes it. This, Gabriel promptly spends on one more round of beer for the house. On last call.

JENNIFER   And seldom is heard
           A discouraging word

15

Gabriel stabbed his hook into the flat back of an alfalfa bale, lifted it on his thigh. The knife-cut stalks bit into his flesh as he pivoted and pushed. On the ground, the bale was quickly surrounded by horn-buttressed heads. Muscular tongues searched into the centre. An upturned horn that should have been sawed off slashed the air and drove into another head, drawing blood below the eye.

The bales off, Gabriel battled in to pull off the strings. Each bale was so tightly clustered he had no place to wedge in. A pilot flying overhead would see something like daisies, brown-petalled, green-centred. From where he stood, Gabriel saw a row of spongey cunts and tails decorated with balls of dried shit. He pushed sideways on the tail hump of an old hereford. She kicked him solidly on the shin. His head jerked down, the cow beside flashed her tail and caught him across the bare neck with the wet and shitty switch. He flipped the hay hook round and laid into both cows, smashing the wooden handle into their backs and sides. He beat his way in between and slugged one in the soft pink nose when she wouldn't move.

Back in the cab with the knot of strings in his lap, he stared at a crosshatch of blooded scratches on his thigh. They grinned up through a frayed patch in his fairly new jeans. I've been here too long, he thought. Ramming the accelerator, he peeled away, leaving long strips of greasy black through the newly green pasture.

When he came in sight of the house, the familiar car in the yard put another peak on Gabriel's anger. He shouted a curse, slammed the steering wheel so hard that the heels of his hands bruised through his gloves. He considered turning around and hiding in a coulee until they left.

The stupid, useless economy car, North America's incompetent answer to Japanese efficiency; it hadn't improved its looks since they'd driven it to Batoche. Rust holes stood out like cruel mouths on each fender. Like a pair of gawking tourists, the two of them stood scuffing the ground by its open doors. Gabriel lurched into the yard, skidded to a stop, marched by into the house. The open door behind him was his only greeting to these friends.

By the time Clive and Phipps entered the house, Gabriel was standing at the stove, lighting a burner under a pot of coffee. Across the broken linoleum was a track of mud and shit. He left them to look the place over: the food-smeared arborite table, a full and spilling ashtray in its centre; dead and dying plants in a limp row along the sooty window sill; a couple of buzzing flies expiring on their backs on the floor; an empty whisky bottle kicked up against the foot of the droning fridge.

"Country hospitality," said Clive, "I've heard about it all my life and now I know it's true. There *is* a Walton's Mountain."

Gabriel kept his back to them, worked sideways to a cupboard.

"How did you know I was here?"

Clive answered while Phipps hovered behind him, trying to get a cigarette lit.

"Give a problem to a man used to following broken twigs through federal Byzantium and you get an answer, my picturesque foothills fart."

Phipps punctuated this with a cough and added, "He bumped into Leona."

Gabriel poured coffee and turned with the cups. He set them down heavily on the table, slopping some over the edge. It drooled down the sides in thick rivulets.

Clive picked one up. "You can tell this is outstanding coffee. The legs give it away."

"If I'd wanted company, I'd've let you know where I was."

"Did it happen to occur to you," said Phipps, "that until Clive ran into Leona we were debating whether to buy a wedding present or have the river dragged?"

Gabriel dropped onto a chair. "My guardians. I feel so fortunate."

"I thought we were your fucking friends."

"Down, Phipps." Clive leaned into their hot eyeline. "You'll have to excuse Phippsy, Gabriel. It's the academic off-season again and he's back watching soap operas. What I think he means is that your old buddies were concerned and thought they would drop down this sunny weekend for a visit. However, if we're interrupting a cracking good depression, we can go again. I know how hard it is to get deep into the existentialist void with others present."

Gabriel dragged his cap off onto the table. The shape of it stayed in the rags of his hair. He slid a hand behind his neck and left a trail of grease, shook his head as if to clear it. "I don't even have a drink to offer you."

"As it happens, Phipps and I anticipated such a thing." Phipps bolted out of his chair, out the door, the car keys jangling.

Phipps was hardly back when Winterspeer came, another case of beer fixed to his long arm. Seeing him in the doorway, Gabriel said, "Christ, another nose for misery."

"Eye, actually. Eye for misery. I was watching you with my telescope as you beat your cows on the south forty. Walter Winterspeer.

Pleased to meet you all, I'm sure."

Clive, Phipps and Walter talked, getting to know one another rapidly, without help from Gabriel. Phipps wanted to know about Winterspeer's background, meaning where he fit into the great puzzle of Western Canadian history.
"Well, Jeffery — if I may call you that — I don't."
"You're from another part of the country then? Or another country? You seem a bit British."
"A sensitive subject for me, really."
"Sensitivity about background seems to be common around here." Gabriel ignored the intended barb.
"The mixture of bloods, I think, Dr. Phipps. German marrying Englishwoman. Russian beldame consorting with American. It is often better just to keep quiet."
Phipps's next beginning was "I don't mean to pry," which sent Clive into gales of laughter and even got a chuckle from Gabriel.
"Inside joke," said Clive. "Phippsy's life work is prying. At the same time it's possible he doesn't mean to."
"I can speak for myself, Ruthven."
"Isn't *that* unfortunately true?"
"Excuse me," said Walter, "I wasn't trying to be coy, actually. It's just that, for my family history, I've taken a sort of revisionist tack. I have a perfectly good one already, I suppose, but, as a poet, I have decided to take on as my major work the devising of a truly great family history that would be a proper gift to my son."
Phipps looked at Walter with a mixture of delight and horror; delight at having found a fellow poet, horror at historical revisionism in any form. Walter continued.
"The answer therefore is that A: I do not fit, and B: I'm not sure where I fit because I haven't finished creating my history yet."
Everyone turned to Gabriel when he made a noise like the start of speech. It was a false alarm.
"Had Gabriel spoken now," Walter went on, "it might have been to comment on my not fitting in here. Before I began devising my family history, my major work was not fitting in. I did not fit in with gusto. I tempted members of this community, again and again, to expunge me by force and thus liberate the good, honest, moral, hard-working local girl who had the misfortune to fall upon my ring.
"But, in Gabriel's long absence from here, something remarkable has happened. I still do not fit in but — and I think you will find this very informative, Gabriel — but I am now tolerated, even treasured, you could almost say. Come on, Gabriel, admit it. Admit you're

intrigued and that you want me to go on."

Gabriel admitted no such thing. Walter went on.

"There is a fascinating mechanism at work in this community. When you first enter here, a foreigner, they do not like you and and they let you know. They also expect you to lose no time becoming like them if you intend to stay. But, of course, if you try to do this, they will never admit that you have succeeded because that would lower the currency of being born here. The effort, however, is still the price you pay for entry.

"For Gabriel, it was even more difficult. Born here, raised here, educated after a fashion here, he was at one time totally accepted — and accepting. When he chose to depart in thought and deed, he became a traitor. His status became like mine, with the added dimension of betrayal."

Walter turned his body fully toward Gabriel.

"The thing you will find interesting, Gabriel, the moral of this long story, is that my years of resistance have earned me a new status. I am now a 'character,' by God, and I will tell you that this strange, conformity-loving society has an equally strong love for its characters. Once you have achieved the status of character, they watch you constantly with jolly looks on their faces, awaiting your next bizarre statement or act. When you have committed it, they're off like greyhounds, tossing it from one to another, embellishing it in the retelling, applying to it the lustre of a legend."

Phipps's area of expertise had been entered.

"A similar phenomenon existed among the Native peoples," he said. "Differences of mind and behaviour, the more bizarre the better, were regarded as a special blessing. The so-called Medicine Man or shaman was often no more than a crazy person."

"I accept the honourable nomen of crazy person."

"I . . ."

"What Phipps is trying to say is that the Medicine Man was a character."

"I know and thank you. What I wonder, Gabriel, is whether they would accept you too eventually. As a character, I mean." Gabriel made another noise like the advent of speech. This time, when the heads had turned, he did actually say something.

"They accept Willy Hinkerman too and he fucks pigs."

The beer in their stomachs began to work its way around their organs, particularly the kidneys and the brain. When several mentioned needing an exit for some of this beer, Gabriel invited them to piss in the yard, having diagnosed a shortage of water in the well. Phipps was momentarily concerned about the effect pissing on the ground might have on the drinking water. Gabriel invited him to the door for a look round the place, to see that the whole valley was "full of shit in one way or another."

Clive liked this idea. Really, he said, when you think about it, isn't that the vile fact of human life? You can soften the water, install taps of gold, invest in a jacuzzi that will spray it at you any which way — but you can't get around the fact that, high in the mountains where the snow and glaciers melt to form the river, a deer is right now standing with its back arched, pissing straight into nature's nectar. Clive thereupon went to the sink, poured out a slightly cloudy glass and drank it off straight. Saying, ahhh.

Walter offered a toast to Gabriel and his friends, all of whom he found to be company of a very edifying sort. Then he spoke on the related subject of Beaver Fever. Beaver Fever, he said, was a serious illness that people who drink the water in mountain passes and lakes had lately been succumbing to. Tourists and those living in the natural glory of the national parks had been reported dropping like flies. Naturalists protested that the poor beaver was being falsely blamed in the sense that many a mountain animal was passing this sickness around via the common currency of water. The naturalists themselves preferred to take chlorinated city water with them on their hikes, or wine or beer. Phipps contributed the vaguely related fact that a populist leader in India drank from what he called "the cystern of life." That is, he consumed a substantial quantity of his own urine every day. The ultimate conservationist, Clive declared the man, raising his glass. The one true recycler. And they drank another toast.

This led eventually to a "tour of the turds." Gabriel led the group from yard to pen and down the valley to the feed and bed grounds. Cow flap, calf scour and horse bun, in all stages of freshness and decay, dampness and dessication, were observed and commented upon. To prevent any upflaring of Beaver Fever, a stream of beer was maintained from a case in the truck.

Phipps begged to be shown the grave of Baptiste and, though Gabriel argued there was nothing to see, Phipps insisted and won. Clive produced a never before unfurled backpack and donned it for the purpose of carrying beer up the steep hill. At the damp, shady burial ground, between the trunks of bull pines, the now sweaty and hard-breathing lot of them beheld the grey afternoon mountains and the closer mound of Gabriel's hill. Pressed by Phipps, Gabriel told the story of Baptiste's grave, but not very well. He concentrated on the mundane work of it; Joe and he digging through roots and rocks, thunking into a shelf of limestone so thick and continuous Hank had finally resorted to a stick of dynamite.

The sun declined and set. Beer gone, the four returned to the house where an argument started about how the evening should be spent. Phipps and Clive were all for going to town. Gabriel suggested poker. When he saw that this idea would not fly, Gabriel offered that they could go up the historic Crowsnest Pass: the Lost Lemon Mine; history of labour strife in the mining towns; bootlegging during the prohibition. They could see the town where the rumrunner Emperor Pic had been hanged for shooting a policeman. Phipps would have a ball.

But Phipps and Clive persisted, arguing that Beaver Creek held the history they really wanted to know: the place where Gabriel copped his first cheap feel; the place where he got drunk on his graduation night and threw up into his date's high-heeled shoes.

"Remember Batoche!" they cried, "Remember Duck Lake!"

"You decide," Gabriel said to Walter who had not stated an opinion thus far.

Walter dithered, finally approached the phone. He picked it up with great trepidation, dialed. He spoke little, listened carefully with the receiver pulled a little away from his ear, set the receiver down.

"Beaver Creek, then," he said quietly, "and may God have mercy on my soul."

16

The beer and the company had brightened Gabriel, though no one would have called him sunny. Improvement to overcast. When the lights of the town reared out of the valley, a different kind of cloud came and rested on him. He said nothing but the other three, crushed into the cab, could tell, the way you feel a storm even though you're in a room without windows.

They drove down the hill to the stop sign and waited there for a gap in the stream of pick-up trucks that seemed endless in both directions.

"Where are they going?" asked Phipps, interrupting the metronome whack of the signal light. There was strain in his voice from the weight of Clive on top of him.

"Nowhere," grunted Gabriel.

"Why?"

"Who knows?"

Walter, seated in the middle and guarding his privates from the gearshift, expanded on this, explaining that the drivers were "maining." They were mostly young, and checking one another out across the midline of Main Street; boys looking for girls and vice versa, enemies looking for enemies, friends for friends. It didn't really end in the sense that, to the west, they reversed themselves in a residential crescent while, to the east, they were turning through a hamburger stand parking lot. Up and down until their gas, money or youth ran out.

Phipps immediately saw an intellectual paradigm: approach and avoidance; isolation in the protection of motion; society at arm's length; consumption of energy as sacrament.

"Knock it off, Phippsy," said Clive, "or I'll wiggle."

When Gabriel finally butted his way onto Main Street, Clive asked that they do a main and that Gabriel perform the function of tour guide. Where exactly did he scrabble drunkenly in the snow at a girlfriend's basement window, hoping to beg forgiveness, only to see her get up to some remarkable mischief in the upright position with another boy? Gabriel said: "This is the war memorial, this is the confectionery, this is the Royal Bank, this is the liquor store. Hey, what the hell did they do with the Co-op?"

"Moved it to a shopping centre north of town," said Winterspeer.

"Jesus."

Turning through the hamburger stand parking lot, they saw a couple of teenage boys pushing on one another's chests. A crowd of other teenagers surrounded them, shouting encouragement. Through the rolled down windows they heard the shouted word "fuckpig!"

"Quick, Phippsy, write it down. Local colloquialism."

Then up the street the other way and Gabriel parked across from the door of the Queen Elizabeth Hotel tavern. He stared out the window as if lost in thought, then asked Winterspeer if he remembered being thrown out that door onto the sidewalk.

"Not a totally isolated incident, I'm afraid."

The time Gabriel had in mind, two Indians had come out after Walter and helped him up. The three had then proceeded down the sidewalk east.

"I do remember. The rascally bartender had refused to accept my cheque."

"I was parked right here, with Dalton and Jimmy, looking for a bootlegger. We even thought about trying to send you back in. You were singing something when you walked away. Sounded like 'Home on the Range.'"

Winterspeer sang for them:

> Oh give me a home
> Where no buffalo roam
> And no deer and no antelope play,
>
> Where seldom is heard
> A horse fart or a bird,
> And the sky is burnt umber all day.

Gabriel snapped off the engine, pulled out the key. "Let's do it."

Something like a thunderclap hit them when they passed through the second door into the tavern: the alternating roar from giant domino speakers flanking a naked, pen-like dance floor. Strobe light. Glitter ball. Records.

At first Gabriel didn't recognize the place at all. At a glance, he did not recognize any of the people either. The four of them moved on to the farthest corner of the room, a bright L-shaped alcove beyond the main room where the only older people huddled.

Scanning again from his chair, Gabriel saw that the bartender, busily winding a towel in a glass, was somebody he had gone to school with. He had been in grade ten when Gabriel had first come to town for grade five. Life in-between had put a permanent scowl on him. At thirty or so, he was already balding and wore a band of suet under his apron. Their eyes met and passed on; no word or nod.

In the dark part of the bar, the faces of what seemed to be children glowed like ghosts, white and Indian ghosts dressed in denim and leather. Some had their hair dyed technicolour and spiked. Gabriel recognized a few family features. She might be a Brenmar; over there, a Siedlitz; that one, a Red Plume. After the beer came, a skinny, tall, unhealthy drunk from their section tottered over and peered at him. You're Gabriel, aren't you, he said? When Gabriel answered yes, the drunk shook his hand with great grip and emotion. Tears welled in the sea that was already around his red-yellow eyes. The drunk said something not altogether comprehensible that amounted to thanks to Gabriel for being Gabriel. Then he staggered back and fell in his seat.

"Who was that?" asked Phipps.

"Haven't a clue."

Something about that exchange caused Gabriel to relax. He told a few stories about this place: memorable drunks, vomits that landed in odd places, a wildman from Christie Mines known only as Wildman who tried to cut down a metal roof support to prove the power of his chainsaw. He compared notes with Winterspeer on what it used to be like here and the fact that it no longer looked that way seemed to please him. Phipps was wearing a particularly glum face over this pleasure taken in history's disappearance and, if he had asked Gabriel why, Gabriel would finally have been capable of an answer. He would have spoken the words "semipermeable membrane" because it had just occurred to him that his passage out of youth had been across such a membrane. Having gone across, the way back was barred by chemistry. Three cheers and thank God for chemistry.

What this notion did was create in Gabriel the sensation of invisibility, or maybe of having a costume so good no one could figure it out. The drunk didn't bother him. He'd seen guys like that in other bars; they made a life out of watching the door swing and keeping a mental register of who went where and how they changed. Being recognized by him wasn't much worse than finding a new kind of junk mail in your box. You are one of five million lucky people to win this fabulous prize.

Buoyed up so high by this idea, Gabriel hardly noticed Phipps and Clive as they declared that they hated this bar. It looked like any tavern anywhere, they charged; the kind of place where Phipps's students went to burn off the brain cells he tried gamely to train into pattern. Gabriel forgot to argue when Winterspeer suggested they go to the Legion, of which he was a member. In the Legion, Walter said, they would find the town's last surviving flavour of rural locale. It had gone there to hide, to grow old and inevitably to die.

The Legion was across the street and down a block, a sandstone edifice. Inside, Winterspeer signed them in with small talk for the guardian of the door. It was then that Gabriel lost his lucky, invisible feeling and met again his darkest unease. He recognized this skinny, grey-headed man at the door; and worse, the man recognized him. "How's it going, Gabriel?" he said. Looking farther, Gabriel saw many more faces he knew; all looking back, all knowing him.

They went in and sat. Phipps and Clive enthused that this was more like it. Darts, shuffleboard, grey hair, polka band, portrait of the Queen in a gilt frame, military insignia and cow brands on the walls.

"Remember Batoche! Remember Duck Lake!"

But Gabriel was thinking that this was neither.

Painfully edgy now, Gabriel watched. Two men, in the most social phase of their drinking, had risen and were moving among other tables, passing along greetings and cracking jokes. "Evening, Walter," said the first of these to reach them. George, thought Gabriel, Baxter. Father an implement dealer, farm south of town, knocked up Audrey Wilhelm; her father tried to run him over on Main Street, or was it in the Co-op parking lot? She'd showed at the wedding.

"And Gabriel, by God! I never expected to see you round these parts again. What rock did you climb out from under, for chrissake?"

Gabriel explained, squashing five years into less than half a minute, that he had climbed from under a rock in Calgary.

"And how's your dad? I heard he'd been kicked in the head by a horse or something. Ambulance took him to Calgary, that right? Anything serious?"

"Nothing serious, just kicked in the head."

An embarrassed pause that finally jarred George Baxter on his merry way. Then Gabriel spotted Dalton and the discomfort distilled into something purer.

Dalton sat with his father and mother, and a woman Gabriel recognized as the adult version of Julie Pritchett. She sat close to Dalton, leaning over practically into his chair. She giggled shrilly, shoulders bouncing. Dalton paid no attention. He was occupied elsewhere, staring at Gabriel.

Five years had given Dalton a worried look, troubled beyond his years. Always thin, he was now too thin and the skin sucked so tight onto his bones, the continual frown, made him seem much older than he was. Gabriel imagined the wedding. Dalton in some funny-fitting tuxedo, a peacock colour. Jimmy standing beside him, paralyzed by responsibility; feeling his pocket over and over where the ring box was, so unsure of himself it seemed possible that even now the ring could leap out and get lost. Dalton continued to stare at Gabriel. Blue eyes; everyone assumes they're attractive but the mean, small ones in Dalton's head looked sick somehow, runny and apt to fade to white. He stood up and his chair flew back, bouncing on the parquet dance floor.

He stuck his thumbs in above his rodeo buckle, hoisted his pants on his skinny bum. He walked toward Gabriel, continuing to stare, knocking a table and not bothering to stop or apologize as the people reached for their slopping glasses of draft.

"Hello, Dalton." Gabriel offered his hand. Dalton kept his thumbs hooked under his belt buckle.

"Why don't you just get out of here."

"Wait a minute now, we've got as much right . . . "

"Shut up, Jeff. Look, Dalton, grab a beer and we'll go to another table."

A jagged trembling started up in Gabriel's old friend. He gripped onto the top of a nearby chair to stop it showing.

"Nobody wants you back here. The trouble with you leaving bastards, you go off for years and then you just waltz back in when you feel like it."

The bar was quiet, the band between sets and nobody playing shuffleboard or darts. Noise would have been merciful and there was no mercy. Dalton's father stood and came hobbling, fighting against the dryness in his joints. Julie had her hand over her mouth and Dalton's mother was reaching for her.

"Free country, I guess, Dalton."

Gabriel watched the hands lower away from the belt and tremble in the fingers.

"Come on, goddamit! Get the hell out or I'll kick your ass out of here myself!"

Gabriel remembered the way this conversation would have continued in the old days. You and who's army? Think you're man enough? He said nothing.

Dalton's confidence was gone.

"You chicken, fucking Halfbreed bastard! Run away or fight!"

Dalton kicked the side of Gabriel's chair. He seemed shocked when nothing happened. Then his father was there, and the legion manager. They took hold of Dalton. He pushed back at them, writhed out of their grip. The legion man appealed to Walter.

"Sorry, Walter. Maybe you gents should go." The legion man tweezed a fin off a roll in his shirt pocket, dropped it beside the jug on the table. "On the Legion, okay?"

Gabriel got up first. Left with Dalton's almost tearful yells bouncing off his back.

Gabriel drove. Coldly sober. There was nothing very funny to say so Clive went to sleep. Phipps, on top of Clive for the return voyage, tried a couple of approaches in his familiar outrage but his words hung in the air, nobody listening. He slumped back onto Clive and let the beer close over him.

After the pavement had been left for the louder rumble of gravel, Walter said, "Jimmy McCrimmon went away a couple of years ago. Drilling activity down here hasn't been brisk. I think he's in Rainbow Lake."

A rabbit veered into the truck lights. Gabriel slowed to its speed. The rabbit, trapped by the light, would go out to the grass fringe then back to the centre as if it had bounced off something solid. Gabriel hit the horn and the impulse shot the rabbit through the wall of light.

Glancing once at the sleeping pair by the door, Gabriel said to Walter, "It's strange, you know, that's the first time he ever called me a Halfbreed and I've known him since before I went to school. I didn't even think he knew."

"I suspect it's just another way to put distance between you."

Gabriel turned in toward Walter's yardlight, coasted up onto the pad of gravel by the house. He turned off the engine. They climbed out the driver's side and, leaning on the truck box, smoked.

"So much for being the local medicine man," said Gabriel blowing smoke over the swarm of stars.

"I wouldn't completely judge by Dalton."

"You know, Winterspeer, I don't want to be here. For five years, I barely thought about the place. But, somehow, now that I am back, sounds stupid, but it's like somebody else went away while the real me stayed here and waited for him."

"If I understand you correctly, I don't think it's strange at all. You probably are one person here, another there. And, since you were this person longer, given the chance, he will predominate."

"What I really wonder, though, is whether you can ever leave a place like this and be any good at being anywhere else."

"Human condition to some extent. Either you fit into the pattern laid out for you by your community, corporation, church — or you rebel. In which case you are in charge of what you become. Life as art form, and not all art is good art. Few have any artistic ability at all which explains why so many retreat into conformity. But it's a little early in your case to give up." Winterspeer flicked his cigarette, a red dot trailing sparks into the grass.

"Will you be going soon then?"

"I can't. Not yet."

"Yes, not yet. Well, Gabriel, shake a paw. I must in to my wife and my portion of guilt. She'll have me doing little chores for a week to pay for this."

Sliding his hand from Gabriel's, Walter turned for the house.

"Winterspeer, would you call Jennifer if you were me?"

"Of course. But I'm not you, old son. So it doesn't matter what I would do."

"I don't even know why I want to."

"But you do apparently want to."

"Yes."

"Then I suggest you put your considerable mind to the question of why and see what you come up with."

17

The blizzard that had blown Gabriel home seemed a long time ago, more than the month it had been. The wind had long since chased the last crusts of snow up the coulees and, across the hills, the green had drawn up under and pushed through the brown. Hank and Lyla still weren't back; a few days had turned into weeks. To pass the time, Gabriel sledge-hammered fenceposts and strung wire to rebuild the enclosure behind the barn. Here, he penned his nurse herd. Half a dozen cows, slow to catch last summer, had to be watched still for signs of calving. He was treating two cases of foot rot with daubs of pine tar whenever he could rope and tie them to the truck bumper. He had one cow with too much milk for her calf and one with not enough. (He persuaded the first with a two-by-four to let the calf of the second suck.) The last was a cow with a blood-crusty string of afterbirth. He knew he should probably go to town and buy some hormones at the vet but, not wanting to make that trip, he plunged needles full of penicillin into her ass and hoped for the best.

He did all this with little thought but with an image of Hank's return. When Hank did return, he would be hungry to find fault. If it were all neat and tidy, there would be less to pick at and argue over, and Gabriel could soon go. Gabriel did his work now, painstakingly, to smooth and grease that moment.

Then Lyla phoned from Calgary and named the day they would be back. Hank's condition was "frail," she said, and what absolutely must not happen was any arguing. Fine, said Gabriel. It struck him that the risk could be eliminated entirely if he left before they got there, but Lyla said no. Gabriel got the message that she, or Hank, or both of them wanted this handing back of the reins to be something actual with bodies present.

Off the phone, back with his plans, things did not seem as safe, or smooth. In particular the word "frail" kept coming at Gabriel. Hank frail. It made no sense. Pacing the kitchen, Gabriel launched the argument that it did not matter if Hank was frail. Lyla certainly wasn't. And if there were things to do on the farm that she was not able to do, they could hire a man. After all the years of underpaying Joe and never fixing a thing, Hank had to have money. Let him spend some for once. From then on, whenever he heard the word frail, Gabriel countered instantly that it was not his problem. The moment they were back, he would go.

The few days between the phone call and Hank's arrival should have been days wished away but Gabriel felt himself hoarding them as a nervousness grew inside. When four days had shrunk to two, the unease had become a swelling that hurt. That night, the second last, he could not sleep. Spread-eagled on his mattress, he stared through layers of dark at the roof beam. He thought back over every step. The storm he'd driven through to get here; the awkward times with Lyla; and then, when she'd left him alone, the way his mind had flipped and flopped — wanting to be a farmer, wanting Jennifer, wanting most to run away before his brain blew out of his head completely and left him grass-rooted here, like the various pieces of obsolete machinery in the yard. Sliding even farther sideways, Gabriel found a new kind of discomfort. Staring at the ceiling beam he felt he had already gone, and had left something undone so important he would falter forever after because of it.

It was the kind of night when sleep comes but doesn't feel like sleep, where possibly his dreams were of lying on his back, staring up, wondering what he was wondering.

Dawn seeped through the cracked window, throwing a spider web of light. Gabriel got up off the mattress, hitched on his jeans and walked downstairs. He went straight into Hank's room and began to go through the drawers of the dresser. He did not disturb the fold of Lyla's underwear, did not change as best he could the tobacco smelling disarray of Hank's things. Wads of bills, a ten-year-old auction list, cuff link boxes, string ties, expander arm bracelets, belt buckles, snoose tins full of things that rattled. He didn't snoop in the letters he found underneath either, letters with women's handwriting on them linked into bundles by dried out elastic bands.

It seemed right that the objects of his search were on the bottom of this drawer, under his father's love letters from other women. A rosary, a few religious medals in a plastic playing card box, and the two pictures that had always been on the piano top.

Gabriel went to the kitchen, dusted back the crumbs and ash. He hooked the cardboard pedestal on the back of one picture. The other was in a folder that stood on its own edges. The one in the folder was a wedding picture: Hank in a shapeless suit, a speckled tie — a brushcut so close that the bone down the middle of his skull showed as a blaze of white. Crossing his concave face was a cocky grin, aggressive in a way all out of sync with the occasion. It was as if he were saying, I've got her now, you bastards; what are you going to do about it? His arm around her waist. Gabriel's mother's eyes were not on either Hank or the camera — the floor maybe, though it seemed she was focussing above it. There was a smile, a sheepish, blushing one, and too pleased for Gabriel's liking.

Gabriel was in that picture too. A clump of cells, busily multiplying into human shape, reason above any other why the moment existed to be photographed. Or that was how Gabriel had seen it since he was old enough to count.

He looked for a long time and when he was finished he knew he did not want this picture. It was too much Hank, his moment. For Gabriel it also bore the unerasable caption "twelve years to live." He closed the folder and laid it down flat.

He turned to the second picture, a black-and-white school photo. His mother in grade eleven, a grade she never finished but one her teachers were probably amazed she'd reached. The small smooth-skinned oval, raised in surprise between the coal black halves of hair. A second before, her eyes had been down, the look probably embarrassed and closed. But, for some reason, maybe because she was pretty and shy, and the photographer had reached into his kit bag of old sayings for one of the better ones, there'd been this sudden change. After she died, the few people who talked about her to Gabriel always used the words shy and good. She was such a good woman, so shy — and no more, as if that were sufficient to describe her. As long as Gabriel had the picture, he would be able to reinflate her to human size.

Later, throwing bales, Gabriel wasn't surprised that the unfinished-business feeling hadn't left him. In fact it seemed to have gained momentum like some kind of racer with his finish line in sight. Fourteen years old again, Gabriel could hear his father's voice barking at his back from the truck. "No goddamn way to throw a square bale. Bust her sure as hell. How many damn times...?" They'd only switched from round bales to square that season but already Hank was the authority. Sitting on top of the load after stacking maybe two bales in place, he was now content to watch his sons do the rest. Joe like a machine: stab, swivel, yank, boost, throw. He also had a machine's lack of reaction to the stream of abuse. But Gabriel, though he also kept quiet, burned inside and hated.

It was two years later, when he was sixteen, and they were working at the same job, in the same unchanging configuration, that Gabriel had finally told Hank to fuck off — if he always knew a better way, why didn't he just do it himself? Hank, without hesitation or doubt, stepped up to Gabriel in the truckbox. Joe was about to toss up a bale from the ground. He stopped to watch. Hank, wearing a twist of unpleasant smile as if genuinely looking forward to something, said, "So you think you're man enough, eh? Well, go ahead."

It was the movie scene in which the hero, or the villain, lets the other take the first crack. And Gabriel believed it. He balled up his hand at his side and was thinking where and how to plant the blow when Hank's fist came up under his chin. It knocked him out of the truckbox and onto the ground. The light came back first as a gold web on swirling blood red. The first real image that returned was Hank, above the side of the truck box, throwing bales. He was convincing in his display that nothing important had happened.

Of being seventeen, the scene that remained was Hank, in the kitchen, always building on the superstition that no victory could ever be won over him. He would tease Gabriel into saying what he thought of the world — politics, economics, religion — and then great barks of laughter or the twist of smile.

"That what they teach you at school? Eleven years of expensive government education and that's the best you can come up with?"

Joe was silent of course; using his already completed education (half of grade nine) to read motorcycle magazines, hunting and fishing magazines, magazines about mercenary soldiers blasting jungle Blacks with guns and grenades and flame throwers you could order through the mail using handy detachable forms.

Gabriel eventually learned that silence from Joe. How to let the bait float by. Then, robbed of his entertainment, Hank had to find something else to do. He would pick up the farm magazines he subscribed to in order to maintain the illusion that he cared about farming, but he would drop them soon after. He would go then into his room to "spruce up;" put on a clean cowboy shirt over a dirty body, slick back his hair with aromatic grease. And then he'd leave, either with no words or with some smart-ass parting shot like, "Think I'll see if there's any itchy tail in town. Better than sitting here with you dreary pair of bastards." And gone, to make a misery of some woman's life. His hobby.

The grubby way Hank talked had always, to Gabriel's ears, included his mother. As a kid he'd believed that his father should not chase women, should mourn. And later, when he'd given up on that idea, Gabriel still believed that, if Hank had any feeling at all about her, he would treat the others as if she were somehow "in" them.

But Hank had his own consistent way of dealing with women. They were one thing to him, generic, a thing to be taken lightly, set at the butt end of jokes, nailed to the bed with his superior cocksmanship. For Gabriel, that was insult without end.

Swinging bales, Gabriel dug down even farther, going below the death of his mother to the very first layer of hate, where he'd learned to do it. The images here flickered, were yanked around some by the hate that kept them in his mind. Did he really remember his father hitting her? Or was it just another loud, one-sided diatribe that ended with something falling or breaking? And hearing "washed out bitch," "don't take care of yourself," "look like shit?" Could a child of six or seven really invent stuff like that? Or maybe he'd made them up later; a trick of mind applied to an ancient truth or a kid's deception; beefing up his case for hatred after she was dead.

There was one home movie, though, that he wouldn't tamper with or question even now, and that was Hank sprucing up and heading for town "before." The same air of escaping to something better, the same scorn for those who stayed behind, even the same sticky sweet grease in his hair and the same reason for going. With this belief went the other, that in this way his mother had been pushed. Toward the fading, down onto the chair where she often sat rubbing one leg up and down, around the kitchen on slippered feet that scuffed because the feet weren't being lifted. The touching of her children that was more and more a series of brushing farewells.

Gabriel pushed cows, pulled strings, checked bags for tightness, felt oppressed by the surround of hills. And he decided he would not wait until tomorrow to go. There was only one way to leave this place after all and that was to cut and run. He didn't owe obedience to Hank, nor politeness to Lyla. As soon as a load of hay was out first thing in the morning, he would be gone. A funnel of dust up the road.

A den for a small animal. That's what the duffle bag looked like inside; full of dirty clothes stuffed in rather than folded, and with a spot hollowed out in the centre where Gabriel slid the cardboard-braced picture. A final yank on the drawstring puckered it closed.

The phone rang.

Downstairs, Gabriel stood in front of the phone and let it ring, hoping it would stop. It didn't and, when he lifted the receiver and said hello, a flood of words poured into his ear. "Gabriel, Joe. Don't say anything. I'm in the Broken Arrow up the Pass and I gotta talk to you. The Old Man...."

"Hank isn't here. Just me."

Joe didn't know what to say. He had rehearsed for one situation only.

"Come on, if you've got something to say, say it."

"What's going on?"

"Hank's in Calgary. Tests on his heart or something. They'll be back tomorrow."

Another silence.

"Joe, for Chrissake, you said you had to talk, so talk."

"Can't over the phone. Somebody'll rubber. Come up here."

"Look, I've had enough of you phoning and telling me what my next move in life is. You want to talk to me, you come down here."

"Can't. I got ... Alice's with me. Alice...."

"Okay, I know about Alice."

"I can't come down on account of her old man. He's real pissed off. He's crazy or something."

"This better be good. Where do I find you?"

"We'll be in the bar."

Gabriel drove to the highway, turned for the mountains; he was soon inside them, the late evening light of the long day still kicking up gold behind the peaks. When the mining towns began, they were one on the heels of another except for the swath of grey stone that had taken out the town of Frank near the turn of the century. Gabriel swerved into the parking lot of one of the old hotels, formerly named for a British royal when miners drank there, now covered with cartoon images of prospectors and Indians in hopes of garnering some tourist trade. The Broken Arrow.

In the far corner of the bar, they sat at a small round table, fenced in by draft glasses and beer nut bags. Gourmet dinner for two. The

Christoff girl wasn't dumpy anymore, had grown up into a top heavy shape amplified by a straining halter top. She coughed and blew her nose as Gabriel sat down, coughed more through Joe's clumsy introduction.

Joe's hair was in need of a cut and a wash. It hung round his face in wild tangles. However the wind had last whipped it, that's how it was. He probably didn't own a comb. He'd also been letting the seven or so hairs sprout on his chin and he looked like he was apprenticing for a job as an Indochinese elder. The other thing Gabriel noticed was that, without the farmwork and his barbells to lift, Joe was getting fat. Over the cowboy buckle of his belt, a sponge of gut had gotten away on him.

Pleasantries aside, Joe asked for money. Gabriel pulled out his wallet and shoved a brown bill across the table.

"That all you got?"

"I'm not the magic teller."

Joe lifted himself, sucked in breath so he could tuck the bill in his jeans. It reminded Gabriel of more of his brother's messy ways. Joe used to have a snap and flap type pouch, the kind that kids chain to their belts; he kept it about a decade after everyone else had switched to wallets. When the stitches went, he threw it away and started to shove everything in his pockets. If he had a driver's license, that's where it would be: in a grey ball at the bottom.

"You want a beer or something?"

Joe would now buy him a night's beer with his own money. Gabriel ignored the draft Joe pushed his way.

"Anything else to say? If not, I'm going."

Joe looked hurt. He reached for Alice's hand and closed his thick, dark-creased fingers over it. Gabriel considered the feeling, the wet of the kleenex she clutched.

Joe was muttering his story. "Guy in town told me there was work at the strip mine, so I came up here to see. The trailer was full of guys. They told us all to fill out applications. I hung around a couple of days and they gave me the same thing to fill out three times. It was fucked. I got work a few days loading a hay truck, that was it."

"Why don't you go back to the farm?"

"You nuts?" Joe laughed, or at least heaved out some air. "You'd like that, eh? Get you off the hook."

"I'm not on the hook. I'm leaving tomorrow morning, regardless. All I'm saying is, if it's work you're after, there's work there."

"Alice's old man would put a bullet in me, no shit. Or Hank.... Naw."

Gabriel sipped from a beer. He nodded toward Alice. "Why don't you take her home anyway? Before she dies of pneumonia."

Alice's head jerked up. Hard to tell if she was crying, the whole face was so puffed and watery.

"Talk to her father."

"You don't know...."

"You getting married?"

"Ya, maybe."

"Tell him that." To Alice: "He won't beat up on you or anything?"

She was shocked, shook her head hard in denial of any such possibility.

"Then go back. Give him a chance to get used to the idea." He took another drink, shuddered. The wet clothes and hair smell of the two was affecting the taste. "As far as Hank, what's it to him?"

"He's really been on my ass lately. It's that Lyla bitch. Come in and changed everything. Besides, Hank'd never let me...."

"You should hear yourself. You sound ten years old."

"Look who's talking. All you ever did was let him run you off. How does that make you a hero?"

They glowered at each other, the trance broken finally by more coughing from Alice and her squirting something up her nose.

"Difference is," said Gabriel, "I don't want to be there. You do."

Joe hit the table weakly. "It's my farm! Or it damn well should be. I do all the work."

"Then go back. Claim it. Hank's not going to be giving anybody much shit by the sounds of it."

"That sick, eh?" Hopeful note.

"What it sounds like."

For a second Joe pounced on the idea of himself with power; then, as quickly, it got away from him.

"Naw," he mumbled. "Not going back. Never change for me around there."

Joe withdrew from the conversation then; he sat back in a dark, indignant brood. Gabriel talked to Alice. It was easier to get her mind off things, probably because she was wishing none of it had happened. But she also had some doomed notion that Joe was her fate. Finally, Gabriel left them to it. He put another ten bucks on the table and left.

Coasting down out of the mountains, Gabriel thought again about the morning and found that the look of his plan had changed. The vision of him scurrying about with bales and chop pails, and jumping into his truck to run, had slipped out of kilter somehow so the person doing these things was not always Gabriel but often the stooping, duck-footed, sponge-gutted figure of his brother. Joe would do precisely what Gabriel had cut out for himself to do, and anytime Joe became a mirror in which Gabriel could see himself, it was probably time to reconsider.

By the time Gabriel rolled to a stop in the yard, it had come down to one peculiar question: if Gabriel were Gabriel, what would he do?

"Gabriel is Gabriel," he said aloud, to the centre of the unlit shape of house. And it was not Gabriel's way to run.

19

The last night. Sleep so far away he didn't look for it. He did count the deck of cards and it was all there. His luck was rotten, that was all. He messed them around on the arborite to play Remember. As soon as he put a card back he forgot where it was.

Joe wasn't the only mirror here. As the night got long, Gabriel started seeing himself other places too, particularly in the dresser drawer where Hank kept the discards in his lifelong game of poker.

"Why don't you call round anymore?"

"Did I do something to make you angry?"

No, but you're on the discard heap anyway, honey. Because that's the way Hank plays. Never save a card: you'll never win but you'll never lose.

And then, Lyla. Was it possible that even Hank had found — how did the Leonard Cohen song go — "the card that is so high and wild, he'll never need to deal another?"

Gabriel struck the cards off the table, a swath on the floor, the backs like scuffed test pattern. A down-at-heel Jack giving him the evil eye; a come-on from a fucked-over Queen of Hearts. He stared up at the phone. Jennifer. That's right; learn to say it right out loud. School day tomorrow. She'd be asleep. Asleep and dreaming about plants in plastic bags, children who couldn't learn — and men. Yes, men; but not Gabriel. Not likely. Not anymore.

20

Gabriel's plan was to be out working when Hank and Lyla arrived. But when he finally did sleep, he slept too long and was still on the yard chores when dust surged behind the shoulder of Baptiste's hill. He sprinted hard and got behind the barn door before the truck rose into view.

When his eyes had accommodated to the dusty half light, he spotted the pitchfork leaning behind the milk stalls. He grabbed it by its smooth handle and, opening a gate, stabbed the tines into the middle of the first box stall. He levered up a stinking thatch and the juicy place underneath released a coil of steam. He carried the forkful of manure along the alley to the back door and, as he passed their stalls, Lyla's Gallant nickered and Hank's less civil palomino batted its ears and showed its teeth. With the loaded fork, Gabriel flipped the latchkey out of its ring and batted back the door. He lofted the manure onto the top of the pile.

Returning along the alley to the stall, the sprays of dusty light through the front wall drew him. He leaned through the motes and aligned his eyes with a crack between boards.

The truck was stopped in front of the house gate and Lyla was already out of the driver's door and circling the front bumper. The cowboy-hatted silhouette on the passenger side did not move. Lyla reached back into the box and brought out a folded wheelchair. She pulled the wheels apart and a plastic seat snapped down. As she knelt to fit the foot stands, the truck door flung open and its corner struck the chair. It jack-knifed, caught a rut and tripped over onto its side, the top wheel spinning. A metal cane with rubber feet probed out of the cab. Lyla was standing now, hands on her hips, arguing into the truck cab. Beneath the open door, Gabriel saw a leg in a walking cast drop down. Lyla leaned in and produced the rest of him.

A sensation like a cap of thistles shoved down on Gabriel. Hank fought Lyla off with his free hand, moved out from behind the door: a bent figure feeling with a cane, leaning heavily on it, dragging the walking cast forward, reaching for a new hold. Lyla followed him closely, her hands raised like someone about to catch a basketball.

Gabriel led Hank's and Lyla's horses out into the corral, let them eat the new grass and weeds beginning to fringe out under the bottom pole. He went back in and shitted out their stalls, right down to the worn and rot-peeled boards. The knots stood out of the wood like bones under the skin of somebody old and yellow. He climbed into the loft and dropped down fresh straw. But when he stepped back onto the ladder, the manger was empty.

From the top of the ladder, he could see the pink part bisecting Lyla's scalp, the surge of grey on either side before the blond began. Her braids swung as she ripped at a moldy brick of straw with her hands. Then she stood straight and kicked at it and he could see her face. He read quickly what was new there. He wasn't sure exactly but it was something big and muscular, compressed to face-size by a gritty, continuous exertion.

He came the rest of the way down, said hello. After awhile she answered. She leaned where he was leaning, a five-foot stretch of hair-polished manger rail between them.

"I'm no doctor. I didn't understand the half of what they told me. But it's no good. All the tests showed things wrong. Arteries all hard and plugged up. They did something called an angioplaste. Knocked him out and pushed a balloon in there that let the blood through. But there was some other thing wrong they couldn't operate on. They kept saying he was lucky to be alive."

Gabriel watched her closely; could do because she wasn't looking at him. He wondered how the Old Man did it. The barflies, that was one thing — stiff prick and no conscience were probably enough qualification there — but his mother, and now this Lyla.

She pushed off the rail, walked back along the alley and outside. He followed until he saw her face along the shiny jaw of her horse. He went back to spreading straw. She passed through a few minutes later, walking quickly by him.

"Lyla."

She stopped, turned.

"I didn't know he was so bad."

"And now that you do?"

"I could stay awhile longer, that's all."

"Suit yourself."

Hank wasn't where he could be seen when Gabriel finally went in. Gabriel didn't look for him. He sat at the table with his boots on and filled an ashtray with smokes from a pack Hank had left on the table. Lyla had brought groceries and a roast was cooking and spitting in the oven. The smell filling the kitchen nauseated Gabriel, as if by living out of cans and jars for so long, he had rendered himself incapable of facing real food. He watched a plum-coloured night collapse around his hill. It was after ten and dark by the time Lyla came back into the kitchen. She pulled the roast out, made gravy, set the table for three. She left again and Gabriel could hear her crossing to Hank's door. He stood then, reached above the stove and snapped the palm braid off the foot of the cross. He took it out to the front step and crushed it to dust under his boot. Coming back, he saw from the porch that Hank was there.

On the far side of the table, his father curled his shoulders to brace himself as he lowered onto a chair. The front of his shirt bagged open and showed a chest like the meat-cleaned carcass of a chicken. He made it down, tipped his head back and said, "What do you think you're looking at?"

21

The first days of June, the first days of Hank's return. Summer heat came and lulled the farm into a drowse. The cattle lay glaze-eyed in their own shit, chewing thin cud with puffs of new green all round them. On the second day of heat, one of Gabriel's late cows huffed out her water bag and then did nothing. He had to bring the pullers and winch out the newborn while she lay as if dead. Hawks on fenceposts. A mating pair of mallards on the spring-full slough frozen as a photograph. A coyote sifting across the hillside, neck curved to keep the house in view, suddenly flopped down panting like a dog; as if to say, "Fine. Shoot me if it's so important."

The earth of the only grain field paled to grey and Gabriel weakly knew the urge to till and seed it. He started the tractor, warmed the oil, drained and changed it. He dragged the cultivator out into the middle of the yard and, for lack of new shovels, moved the old ones around. The ones worn to thin boomerangs, he switched to less demanding spots on the frame. He brought the seeder in beside the cultivator; scraped the bars of moldy grain from the base of the seed boxes, poked mouse nests out of the downspouts, squeezed grease into the machine's various nipples. But he did all this as slowly as the cows chewed cud and had no will to take the further step onto the land.

Inside the house, something boiled and brewed, and Gabriel was content to let it steep. He tinkered and waited on the Old Man.

Hank slept a lot. In the afternoons, Lyla pulled a chair onto the step for him to sit. He stared at the hills, he rubbed his knuckles; finally, he launched out of the chair and inched around the yard and buildings, poking his cane into things. But, through all of this, his eyes and feet skirted widely the places where Gabriel worked.

Lunch and supper were the only times they faced one another directly. Across the table, Hank's questions were about the farm at first. He had to repeat himself to keep up the illusion of something being said. Then, after a couple of days, he added the odd question about Gabriel; carefully impersonal ones. Was he finished university? What would he do when the gas ran out? When Gabriel said they were still finding quite a lot and that it wasn't likely to run out in his time, Hank did not argue. And that was strange enough.

Then, on their fifth evening back, Lyla came into the kitchen after supper. She told Gabriel that Hank wanted to talk. As Gabriel passed her, she reached and touched his sleeve.

The Old Man was in the armchair. He looked boneless, like

something loose that had been thrown there. The face was cinched up square, though, and wore disapproval Gabriel was meant to see. Gabriel sat down on the other side of the room, on the cushioned end of the couch near the piano. He was still waiting and watching as the lips clicked apart.

"What did you do with the picture?"

"I'm taking it with me."

"In plain English, you stole it."

"I don't have one of her. I'll get another one made and send it back if you want."

"You had no right."

"I'd say I had quite a lot of right. I didn't look at anything else, if that's what's worrying you."

It wasn't funny, particularly, but Gabriel did have an urge to laugh. A short course in how Hank did things. The picture wasn't the issue at all, just the left jab that set up the haymaker.

"Wasn't right," Hank said, "but, since you've got it, send *me* the original and *you* keep the copy."

"Whatever." Gabriel moved as if to get up.

"Wait."

The Old Man rearranged himself.

"In case you haven't noticed...." He broke off and started over. "Since we're talking about your mother, I might as well tell you. It was her farm and I've decided that, after I kick off, it's yours — and that chicken bastard Joe's. If you know what rock he's under, tell him. But I want Lyla looked after. House is hers. And a share of the income. Twenty percent. Plain enough?"

"What makes you think Joe or I want anything to do with this place?"

"I don't care if you do or you don't. It's not for you I'm doing it."

A burning on Gabriel's cheeks, the skin feeling tight across his cheekbones. From the corner of his eye, he could see Lyla. She was leaning under the arch but not facing their way. Listening rigidly. Gabriel got up, passed her, left.

At the junction between the gravel and the highway, Gabriel hit the brakes and the gravel rolled under his tires. The choice of right or left stopped him dead. He looked up the highway, at the darkness gobbling the yellow line. He could go that way: the Crowsnest Pass and Joe, if he could find him. He'd probably moved on from the Broken Arrow by now, proving Hank right. He *was* a chicken bastard; he *was* hiding under a series of rocks. If Gabriel did find his brother, Joe would probably ask for a prognosis. Week, month, year? If I came and let off a shotgun by his window in the night, do you think it would hurry him along? Gabriel looked down the highway: Beaver Creek and Jennifer. He saw his own reflection in the outside rear view, greenlit by the dashlights. If she saw that hovering outside her window, she'd have every right and reason to pull the blind and lock the door.

The engine drummed, the headlights poked out across the highway and saw nothing but the fence beyond the opposite ditch. Once in a long while someone else's headlights appeared, one light splitting into two. When the car or truck shot through the wedge of his own light, he tried to guess the make and year. Then the engine started heating, the needle creeping up on red. He backed onto the shoulder, shut off the engine, sat in the quiet and the dark.

22

Gabriel pushed the clutch and coasted, down into the farmyard and up again to the house. He switched off the engine and watched.

The way the noon sun flowed over the house its parts were almost colour-coded, varying shades of grey and sad yellow. The firm small centre belonged to Baptiste, his homestead shack. The additions to that centre, slumping away and standing on top of it, looked haphazard by comparison. Hank's additions.

When he'd married and got rid of Baptiste to town for a time, his first act was to build a new bedroom for his wife and himself: the square jutting out at Gabriel now. Then the milk separator porch went on: the cube to Gabriel's right, sloping slightly to the front step. When Baptiste got too crippled to live alone, another room was tacked on, to the back. And when the kids were too big to camp out in the living room any more, Hank got really industrious: a second storey.

Shortly after that "it" happened, whatever "it" was. With the second storey walled in and roofed, and a steep open staircase built down one end of the living room, Hank lost interest — forever. With the tools and wood shavings still out on the plywood floor, all carpentry upstairs ceased. Two mattresses were dragged up and flopped down between the raw two-by-fours, and so it stayed: an uninsulated hole to which Joe and Gabriel were vanquished after a certain hour of every evening to fight over quilts in search of warmth.

The only relevant evidence, a remembered conversation:

Baptiste saying, by way of a joke, "At least you could give them kids some bear grease to rub on themselves."

And Hank replying, "None of your goddamn business, old man."

He's in there somewhere. Probably one step back of his bedroom window, watching.

Gabriel looked away. In the part of the corral that stuck out from behind the barn, Lyla's horse stamped and shook its mane, trying to get rid of a fly. Finally it moved and stood tight to the length of Hank's palomino, its head by the other horse's ass. Each horse's tail keeping the head of the other clear of flies. Marriage of convenience.

When Gabriel next looked at the house, a green eyelid had closed over Hank's window. Below the window, a pile of beer cases stood, or dissolved might be a better word. The cardboard had weathered to such mush the cases looked grown together. A river of bottles spilled like brown guts from the side.

In Gabriel, a different set of memories triggered: the place at night, heads in every window, cowboy music and shrieks of mad laughter pulsing out. Gabriel stays outside as long as he can but, when he does go in, a drunk accosts him, holds him pinched by the shoulder and says, "Hank's sure one hell of a good guy." Between swigs from a glass of whisky, adding, "He's a real card, your old man." Probably while the card himself was out pissing against the wall or leaning an aging belle of the ball over a manger rail.

"He's a funny bastard, that Hank."

The trouble being that they got it all, the cronies and the girlfriends. What was left of the great entertainer when the last of them departed was someone sore of head who yelled, "Clean up this fucking mess!" everytime they came too close, as if they'd made the mess in contravention of one of his strictest rules.

But then the crunch comes and not one of these cronies is around, not one is asked to be around. Suddenly a son is more important. The words of last night's speech coming back. "Not for you I'm doing it." (Who then? And why tell me if it isn't?) "Since we're talking about your mother..." Yes, of course. Speaking of Gabriel's mother, which they never did, hardly a word since she'd gone into the ground; but speaking of her now — in riddles — he wanted to do the right thing by her. How else could he have noticed the missing picture so quickly? He'd gone in there to look at her, maybe shed a tear or two on her black-and-white face. As he planned his own forgiveness. The only hitch was that, to actually gain that forgiveness, he had to tell someone who counted. Even a bad Catholic, a convert for the sake of marriage, knows that confession must have its penance, and its tests of contrition. Hank needed someone to witness his prayer, if he hoped to get a clean bill of soul.

Sitting in the truck a great weakness sifted over Gabriel. It came on the cool breeze through the window and seemed to fill every line of the skin that was and wasn't his mother's father's skin. And then, as if she'd been privy to his thoughts and waiting for them to finish, Lyla ran from the house with his duffle bag slung over her shoulder. She threw the bag into the truck box and jumped in the cab beside him.

"Drive until we're out of sight."

"The picture?"

"What picture?"

"There's a picture in my bag."

"I didn't touch it. Come on, get moving — please." Gabriel jerked the gearshift back and down, reversed fast by the cultivator and seeder. He swapped into a forward gear and pounded the gas peddle. Up and around the curve of the hill. Out of sight of the house, he stamped the brake and turned off the engine. It kicked a few times before it died.

"I was going anyway," he said.

"I know. I just didn't want another fight. He was wild after you left. I had to practically ram the pills down him." Gabriel looked over at Lyla, felt for a second that he'd like to put a hand on her. But that big, slightly awkward body, filling one of his father's shirts so the seams were above the points of shoulder — she didn't seem particularly in need of touching.

"Look, Lyla, I gave it a try, okay? It's just history, that's all. Nothing to do with you."

She hit the metal dashboard. It gave back a metal bong. "Man oh man, does this farm *ever* stink of pride! To high heaven! Put three men under a roof with no women and that's all you'll get, every time."

"If it makes any difference, I agree with you."

"Then why?!"

"Because I'm proud."

"Well I wouldn't be if I were you. There's a good man back there going to die a pretty lonely death. How can anybody be proud of that?"

"You don't know what went on. If Hank's a good man to you, that's fine. But he shit in the old nest real deep, believe me."

She jabbed a finger hard into Gabriel's shoulder.

"Listen, you. Go off with this much under your saddle. Your father *does* talk about your mother and not to compliment himself either. I also know there were lots of women after she died and that he was mean with you, but that's just how he happened to mourn her. He still feels damn bad."

Gabriel wheeled down his window, stared at a brown-eyed susan growing above the rock cut on the hill.

"Too bad he didn't feel bad before she died."

But he was talking to the air. The door was open. Lyla was walking away down the road, kicking gravel ahead of her.

Friday afternoon. 3:30. An explosion of children out the double doors of St. Tom's. Children was what they looked like too, even the oldest ones. The town kids cleared off rapidly; the farm kids lingered awhile before boarding their buses. Gabriel remembered the feeling; they would be bitten by envy, those farm kids, as they watched the others go. Town boys after town girls, headed for the coffee shop for a little knocking of knees and sweaty hand-holding under the gum-corrugated table. Feeling out the message: after dark in the park. Meanwhile, the farm kids are off down the blacktop, then onto gravel. The open windows of the bus suck dust. The five-day holiday is over and a weekend of work lies ahead. Thinking about what they're missing plus the ass-jolting motion of the bus teases up some awful hard-ons and the truly desperate find ways to appease them. This was the kind of creature Jennifer Owchenko first put together with the name Gabriel.

Within fifteen minutes the school was empty of children and the first teacher popped out the door: a blond weight-lifter in a straining lime green golf shirt. He ran to his car as if pursued. Gabriel could see the heads of golf clubs sticking up in the back of the station wagon and imagined him on the golf course smacking the pill three hundred yards, each drive crushing another student's head.

The others were slower to get away. Elderly Mr. Coss, who got confused by his own math and physics problems. Sally Anderwazy, who despaired of the lack of love for English literature in this school and town. Others Gabriel did not know. They stopped to talk, perhaps to plan a rendezvous at the Legion. Then Jennifer, alone. They called and waved to her. She waved back, but was not part of them.

She did not see Gabriel and he did not call to her. Watching, Gabriel was bushwhacked by Jimmy McCrimmon's childish voice, saying, "ripe fruit." He hadn't invited the memory, didn't want it, mainly because the ripeness, the plum fullness had passed. She cradled books to her breasts and, leaving the lee of the school, was lashed by a gust of wind. Her raincoat twisted around her body. When she was gone, he left the curb and drove in the other direction.

Halfway down the hill, he passed the teenagers again, the goofing around now escalated to senseless pushing and pulling, anything to get their hands on one another. He took a left and coasted down onto Goose Alley, where the Halfbreeds used to live, back when people called them that and made no apology. He passed an old-timer on the Alley, driving his cane downtown along a route that, for him, must be as time-layered as a river bank. Gabriel looked at everything and tried for memories that would make this simple. But an argument went on nonetheless. It would be so easy just to drive away.

Then he was on her steps, the three down, the lawn at neck level. He knocked, and she pulled back a pleated curtain and saw him. The curtain swung back and seconds passed before the door opened. She had freed her hair of the clasp of pins and wore an outfit of denim and leather. She might even have been wearing a few things in common with that other Friday — which supplied Gabriel with his opening gambit. He asked her if she wanted to go to Lethbridge. She did not smile nor answer, just stood back to let him in.

She left him there, standing inside the door. The porch alcove opened into a narrow kitchen. She stood between the table and fridge, brushing out her hair. Finished, she slid the brush onto the counter and reached for the handle of the fridge. The hand jerked away and she walked off through the living room and into her bedroom, pushing the door by.

Gabriel still did not move. He searched what he could see of the apartment for something, not sure what. Decorative magnets, plastic beetles, trapped papers to the fridge: a newspaper delivery card, this month's schedule for the local cinema, handwritten notes he was too far away to read. He did not move closer. The wooden table was the same one. It had flip-up halves at both ends and only the far one was raised. He took it to mean she had no lover. He went and sat in that place and it felt like an intrusion, as if he'd reached into the fridge and eaten a leftover.

His back was to the living room now and her approach was so quiet he started when she passed. She went to the counter and felt under a plant. She watered it with a drinking glass she kept beside the taps. Then she turned to face him, her arms folded up under her breasts. He imagined without thrill their weight in his hands. He saw too that her eyes were red but only anger remained of whatever had reddened them. He thought she would tell him to go and when she asked if he wanted a beer the sound of the words was no different than if she had.

His lips parted with a sound like scotch tape peeling. Tongue of wood would not speak. She yanked the fridge open, drew out two cans and set his on the table. She flicked the tab on hers and drank. Gabriel's hand groped at his shirt pocket, forgetting he had no cigarettes. Even seeing he had none, she said, "I don't let people smoke here anymore. I don't like the smell."

He did think of going then. The "chock" of his beer can opening surprised him. She had reached and done it.

"You really hate me."

She snapped up the other leaf of the table and sat. "I could get to."

Her eyes went to the high small window below the ceiling and, somehow, her looking there made audible the sound of grit hitting it. Wind and sorrow. The wind rising this morning should have told him not to come.

"I heard about your father. I'm sorry."

"Then you're probably sorrier than I am. I didn't come to talk about him."

"I imagine I know what you came for."

A roasted feeling in the cheeks.

"I should have written," he said. "I'm sorry."

Her beer can hit the table and a cough of froth spat out the hole.

"Oh stop it. Next thing you'll say some clodhopper thing like 'I'm not one for writin' letters.' I wasn't waiting at the post office if that's what you think."

"I didn't think that."

She stood an elbow on the table edge and bounced the back of her hand lightly against her lips. Her eyes were on the table's centre. At his end, Gabriel was looking at her other hand, flat on the table. He imagined putting his hand over it but instead dug his fingernail under the head of a wood screw and pulled until there was pain. He stood up.

"I guess it was a mistake."

"I knew you'd come eventually."

"Who told you I was around?"

"Everybody. It's been a hot item."

He passed her to the door but realized he still had no will to go. It was humiliating not to.

Her back to him, she said, "What did you think? That I'd throw my arms around you?"

"I don't know. I tried not to think about it much."

Her head bobbed as if to music.

"Sit down."

He returned to the chair. Student ordered to his desk. Whipped dog.

"You going away for the weekend?"

She ignored the question. Her eyes came up to his and something hurt flew past behind them, disturbing but not changing the anger.

"I don't hate you. I haven't felt much of anything about you in years. Seeing you here makes me mad, that's all, since you so obviously want something from me."

"I love you."

"You don't even know me."

"I'd like to."

She swung her head, sweeping this aside.

"I'm not just angry at you either. I'm pissed off that seeing you all fucked up about something makes me want to help. It shouldn't be my problem."

"I thought we could spend some time together, and see."

"See what? Listen: I'm not looking for anything or anybody. I'm okay the way I am."

Jennifer was going away for the weekend. She had planned a weekend alone in the mountains and had all her gear packed from the night before. When conversation failed, Gabriel helped carry the boxes out. She was in the van and he was back in his truck, and there it would have ended, except that the engine of the van was slow to start. While the engine rolled, Gabriel climbed out of his cab, took his duffle and carried it to where she was parked. He threw the bag in the side door and climbed into the front passenger seat. The van engine had by now caught but Jennifer kept her clutch foot down.

"Gabriel, what the hell are you doing?"

"I'd like to come with you."

"No."

He did not move. She reached up and scratched at her hairline in front, brought that hand down hard on the steering wheel.

"You're forcing me to be a bitch. I don't want to be. But I don't feel like throwing my life wide open to you, either. Can you understand that?"

"I'm different than I was. I want you to know me. I'm not expecting anything else." He had been speaking to the windshield, now he turned to her. "I'll make a promise: if I'm irritating you in an hour from now, or if you're just sick of it and you want rid of me for whatever reason, stop and let me out. I'll hitchhike back."

She did not look at him or answer for several dead seconds in which the van engine thrummed and gently rocked the chassis under them. She held her hand open in front of her as if she were reading the answer off her palm.

"I'm taking you exactly at your word. And, until we're out of town, I want you to get your head out of sight." She laughed. "And not in my lap."

"Since when do you care . . . ?"

"Don't irritate me, remember?"

"Sorry."

Gabriel jammed down onto the floor and watched the grey blur of pavement through a bend in the base of the door.

For the first fifteen miles beyond town, they did not talk. She had taken the south highway that led either to Waterton National Park or to the U.S. border. The land rolled under them, the grey purple constant of the mountains coming out to meet them the farther south they went. Jennifer kept her eyes forward and both hands locked to the same place on the wheel. Her honey-coloured arms were sleek back to their disappearance in rolled sleeves. The wind in through the window tried and failed to wrap her hair.

When he wasn't watching her, Gabriel looked at the passing fields and pastures: the eye of the farmer he'd recently been. Close to the fence, a sturdy steer calf stood splay-legged beside an indifferent mother, mouth in the dust trying to lick up a flaccid nipple. On the poll of its head, two spools of burned bone. A week or two ago, a heated iron had twisted there.

For a second, Gabriel's thoughts split fore and aft. Ahead he saw himself butting a determined indifference, an old pain in his own head. Behind, Hank was telling Lyla, "He could have at least branded the calves. We'll have to rent a squeeze to do those big bastards now."

Jennifer brought him back. She rolled up her window to be heard and, pointing at a candy-striped smokestack poking above the next hill, said, "Is that it then? Your future?"

Following her eyeline to the foot of the mountains where his old plant stood, Gabriel took stock of the changes. The stack was bigger, looked higher even than the emission standards required. The farmers down here really had them whipped into shape. And a prilling tower to keep the sulphur dust down.

"Yes," he said with firmness. "Not that plant but a processing outfit somewhere."

"That's what I meant." She looked at him and, for the first time, smiled. "For an engineer, you don't add two and two very well."

"Why do you say that?"

"I hate that plant. I belong to an association that goes out and blockades roads to stop them from drilling new wells in wilderness areas."

"Your privilege, I guess."

"And that's what you say when you're with your bosses, of course."

"I say you guys heat your homes with gas same as I do. You drive cars."

"But still you think you'd like a woman who says she'd rather walk and put on a sweater."

"What happened to the idea that love conquers all?"

She rolled down her window again.

At the Waterton park gates, Jennifer bought a season's pass and stuck it to the inside of her window. The van climbed above the first lake, the broad blue expanse below whipped into lace by the wind. Over the river bridge, past the golf course and the cemetery. With the Prince of Wales Hotel rising above them on its rock, Jennifer pulled to the side.

"What's wrong?"

"I don't want to go into town. I just realized that."

"You're the driver."

She flipped the bus around and started back, recrossed the river and took the left that led to Red Rock Canyon. The June sun was still high above the mountains as they travelled the narrow highway west. The landmarks asserted themselves on eye and memory. A gnarled explosion of stone the colour of dried blood briefly surmounted by a toffee-coloured peak. The valley's south face already baking bare in the sun while the north face glowered in shade. The black-green of spruce and pine striped by intervals of younger green where the avalanches travelled. Gabriel noticed patches of reddish dead in the forest and asked her about them. Pine beetles or dessication, she said; the wilderness association was arguing with the park about which. The park said beetles and wanted to log out the dead trees to prevent fire. The association was just as sure it was dessication and held the view it had to burn; nature's way of dealing with the problem.

At the road's end, the parking lot was empty. Half a dozen mountain sheep, patchy and shedding, came up to bum. Noble as dogs. Putting on a small hiking pack, Jennifer yelled at the nearest ram to "Fuck off!" It didn't. It looked back at her with such stupidity you could imagine the horns continuing to spiral in under the hair, joining in a boney knot in the middle. She yelled at the ram again and threw a rock. If it had lowered its rack and knocked her down, she would have been happier.

On the forest path to Blakiston Falls, Gabriel walked behind and watched Jennifer closely. She leaned to part the beargrass over a pale strawberry blossom, pointed into the crossed chaos of deadfall where alpine lilies were blooming. She nudged the unfurling hellebore, its tropic leaf exploding out of itself. With her boot, she smeared fresh bear shit on the path and told Gabriel to keep his eyes open. He imagined he could see the traces of chalk and book lifting off of her the farther into the forest they went.

When they came to the falls, she led him down a stairway that ended in a wooden platform above the water. No one was around and they let their legs dangle, watched the water crush through the neck of stone for a long time. After awhile Gabriel could almost feel the powerful licks the water gave the stone, that smoothed it and wore the undercuts.

His head filled with the sound as the sun inched down, was crossed by igniting clouds. Jennifer took bread, cheese and fruit from the pack. They ate it all, slowly. The end of the valley filled with shadow; the black swept toward them. Uncertain, Gabriel got up from her side and slid down behind her, one leg on each side, his front to her back, and looking out over her shoulder. They stayed that way as the blackened mountain took its first nibble of the circle of sun, then larger bites until all the gold had been devoured.

Back on the road, Jennifer pulled to the shoulder on a height overlooking the valley's campground. Cars with heaped luggage racks and camper vans lined up at the entrance. Beyond the gate, the vehicles crawled along the pavement maze to their assigned spots in the trees.

"I know it makes the best sense," said Jennifer. "It doesn't look like any fun though."

"Couldn't we trespass somewhere? You wilderness types have secret spots, don't you?"

"We don't like showing them off. Someone might see an ooze of oil and decide to drill a well."

A two-seater sports car with a nervous-sounding engine wheeled round the blind curve and jigged left to avoid them. The driver hit his horn and found time to show his middle finger out the back window.

"I promise. Even if a gusher starts up under my foot."

"Okay. We'll see what we can find."

Against the flow of RVs, Jennifer left the valley and then the park. On the road to Belly River and the U.S. border, as the van growled up a steep grade, the sun burst back in on them; sunset reversed. The road swelled into a lookout and Jennifer pulled off. Gabriel reached beer out of her cooler and they drank with the sun downing a second time. Having touched her to these changes a first time, Gabriel ached to do so again. He turned from the view and the low sun streaming over his shoulder painted her such a colour, such a glorious honey-gold, he felt weak.

She laughed at the way he looked at her, and said, "You really do have it bad, don't you?"

"Isn't there some Cohen song you always played. Something about 'win me or lose me, it's this that the night is for.'"

She laughed harder.

"I wasn't trying to be funny."

"I know, baby. But you forgot a couple of things about the song."

"What?"

She sang: "*It is this that the darkness is for.* But the funny part is that it leads up to *Oh, Lady Midnight, I fear that you grow old. The stars eat your body* . . ."

"Ah, shit."

Her arm was across the seatback; she moved her hand onto his shoulder.

"It's okay. You trying to quote poetry is pretty sweet even if you get it wrong."

The hand stayed. He dreamt it moving.

"I was supposed to come back all educated and sophisticated. There wasn't supposed to be a gap between us anymore."

"That's because you saw me as standing still. Time marches on for everybody."

Sudden shadow. The sun had gone again. She flipped her empty to the back and started the engine.

At the summit the road curved east. They passed under a fire tower.
"I applied to be a fire look-out a couple of years ago," she said.
"Jesus. Loneliest job in the world. Why?"
"Teachers. You get panicky thinking it's all you'll ever do."
"You're a good teacher."
"Hmmm."
"If it hadn't been for you, I'd still be on the rigs."
"I know I'm a good teacher. That has nothing to do with it."
"But why a fire look-out?"
"I'm used to my own company. I even like it."
"Do you really want to live like that?"
"Meaning, I suppose, without a man."
"Ya, meaning that."
"Let's just enjoy the scenery, okay?"

She cornered off the highway, heading north this time, back through private land, ranches and gas wells. Gabriel had done some relief switching here and knew the roads.

"I thought we'd stay in the mountains."
"Nature doesn't begin and end there."
"Just about. If natural means wild."
"There's little bits of wilderness everywhere, if you know where to look. People in your business tend not to."
"I wish you wouldn't talk like that. 'People in your business.' I'm not a scout."
"Okay — if you stop calling me a wilderness type."
"You're funny. I don't know if I'm winning or losing."
She drove another mile before she said, "I don't know either."

The road led them past a pumping station, a small plant to boost pressure for the uphill ride to the main plant farther north. Gabriel remembered sopping oil with boxes of rags from the foot of its leaking compressor. Then briefly, they were on blacktop again: the Cardston highway. Jennifer flicked on her lights and, by the time she took a south side road, the lights had begun to tunnel. The road ran out in a cul-de-sac of barbwire, no hunting and no trespassing signs on all sides. A gate to the left, its swing stick wired, gave onto two greasy tracks in a cow pasture. Gabriel was about to go open it when Jennifer doused the engine. He looked at the place afresh.

"Very beautiful indeed."

"Oh, shut up. There's a lake over the hill. If the farmer hasn't had his cows in shitting all over it, it's a nice place."

Opening his door to the west, Gabriel felt the relief of no wind. No wind, no sorrow. They walked to the fence and ducked through tight strands.

Through ankle deep tussocks of grass they walked to the crest of the low hill. Beyond its narrow roof, the lake was pink and powder blue, soaking up and giving back every bit of the nearly failed light. Jennifer nudged him on the arm and pointed.

On the far side of the lake, at the border of faint light and thick shadow, a bull moose slushed in the shallows. Its face ran with water from a mouthful of sloppy green. Its rack swung and the chewing stopped. Slowly it waded away into the envelope of dark.

They continued to the water's edge. Gabriel squatted and lowered his hand in.

"I think I'll go in for a minute."

"The water? You're nuts."

"Call it a bath. The only thing that smells like cow is me."

"Be my guest."

He got out of his clothes, piled them on his boots. He waded in, the cold a pain rising. He stopped.

"Change your mind?" She sat on shore, hugging her legs.

"There any barbwire in here I should watch out for?"

"I've been in. It's okay."

He dove forward then, got it over with. He thrashed out a few strokes and felt for bottom. Country-boy swimmer, he hadn't mastered much more than what it took to cross a pool in a prairie stream. He flipped onto his back and rested, the one maneuver he could sustain. A sound boomed against his ears — the moose coming back? But, raising his head, he saw that it came from behind. Brief photograph of woman, bending to slowly cleave the water. She swam out near him and stood, sculpted head on calming water.

He walked across the soft, weeded bottom, stopped a few feet away. He heard in his head what might have been her thoughts. Actions have meanings. Actions have consequences. It's more than a dance.

The conversation was lagging behind events. The water opening and closing by increments so small, the movement could not be seen. And whose movement? That too could not be told from the slowly closing span.

The touch, when it came, was not like the touch of flesh. Too numbed by cold as if nature had designed a compromise. We are touching, not quite. We are still without decision. But the lips, naked in the air, meeting lightly, spoke the necessary word.

They walked from the water, feeling the weight of gravity heavier on the flesh that emerged, and the weight, voting silently, drew them down on the grass. Her thighs opened and surrounded his body. The hands exploring found the skin taut with cold, fingered it back into pliancy. He stood back on his knees and grazed her hair with the backs of his knuckles, finding in the folds the more velvety wet. She pushed his hand aside and reached with her body to take him, stiffening at the mixture of pleasure and pain. She drew him down and he burrowed round into the nape of neck and the wet press of hair. By his ear, he heard her pleasure searching for itself in him. When he felt the pod inside swell and no time to talk about it, he moved to pull away. She whispered, "No," and brought him back. He stayed with her then, to the end of him, and the end of her.

In the wake of desire, certain facts came hounding. It was cold. They were naked. Soft barbed at this early date, but still there, was a thistle under Jennifer. They got up out of the grass and carried their clothes back to the van. Under the quilt of its bed, shivering warm, Gabriel could feel her thinking. She held herself somehow away and he knew that she was still not won. Only the contest had been made real.

Sitting up, Jennifer asked, "Would you mind if we drove more?" And over his saying he did not mind, she added, "I want to tell you some things."

Back in clothes, the heater pumping cold then warm, she drove and he waited. The park gates went by again and then the solitary lights of ranch country; coming, going. They were as far as the Twin Butte post office and community hall before she began the story.

It was about her marriage.

"You don't know any of this because I used to think it wasn't important. I thought that, if there was something unpleasant in your life, you should just ignore it, forget it. Take the piece out, jam the ends together. Now, I don't know. It seems like life is too short already without doing that."

The husband was a teacher too, met at the end of her last university term. Earnest, active, polyglot sportsman, handsome in a ski-sweater sort of way. A whirlwind summer romance, a great deal of hiking; sex in zipped together sleeping bags. Hardly time to catch their breath before it was time to line up jobs for the fall. Everyone wanted the handful of city jobs available and they saw in the rural ads a chance to keep what they'd started going. When they were accepted for jobs in the same northeast Alberta school, they thought themselves exceptionally clever.

That week, they agreed to tell their respective families about the upcoming common-law arrangement. But when they next got together, both had to confess failure. A long conversation later they were engaged, and phoning their parents back to announce late summer wedding plans.

Sensible, this, they told one another, and sensible further to be able to live in orderly, above-scrutiny fashion in the new town. Start the career on a good footing. And indeed they were the special darlings of their two families and of their new home town: such a handsome, vigorous, newlywed, up-standing young couple. Pulses quickened just at the sight of them.

"But not yours, I take it."

"You've got it."

First of all, it was the mutual rejoicing in nature that failed. Jennifer continued her hobbies of photography and species hunting. But she started to understand that, for him, hills were tall things to be climbed up and skiied down, the faster the better. Lakes were surfaces on which to play hockey and, later in the year, on which to master the all-new art of windsurfing; the board purchased by special order from California, the first such board in the province, he proclaimed, right or wrong. When he wasn't zooming around on top of local lakes, he was pulling pike out of them by the basket which, history's huntsman, he handed over to her proudly for cleaning and gutting and freezing in the new ten-foot freezer. How lucky you are, the local ladies said over interminable coffees, their way of proclaiming and making safe their own desire. Her absolute lack of jealousy was an early warning signal.

During the evenings of that spring, often on into the night, they drafted plans for a house and, during the summer, they built it. Together of course with Jennifer wielding square, saw and hammer. Her husband's turn to hear from the local men how lucky he was. By fall, it was unfinished but livable and, on the yet bare plywood floors, the first open fighting began — about teaching.

He taught on the assumption that all kids love sports. He would take a basketball and show off in the gym for half an hour doing hook-shots and jump-shots and tricky lay-ups. Then, when the students were all worshipping him sufficiently, he would take them back to the classroom to define in mathematical equation the path a fifteen foot set-shot would take from his hands to the hoop. He let each student measure him, personally.

And most of the students did love him. Some even learned math. But, in the unfinished living room full of bought-on-time furniture, Jennifer asked, but what about Paula, and what about Billy, and what about any other kid who didn't know a hook-shot from a left-hook, nor care?

What came out of him then was a brand of social Darwinism Jennifer genuinely hated. She'd been disliking him over small things but now there was actual hatred. Extending these moments, she saw him as a a principal, saw him as a local politician, saw him as formerly married, then, quickly, married again.

"Sound like good reasons to me."

"My side of the story, of course. When I left he was incredibly hurt, not that I imagine it lasted long. But he really was. Kept talking about kids, what great kids we'd have. That seemed to be his greatest concern. Even when he was trying to make it all right again, he still couldn't quite get me in the picture, as anything more than a prime heifer awaiting her moment to bring forth his superior young."

"And I didn't know you much better, is that it?"

"No. You had a lot better excuse. We both did. The young don't dwell on the past and you gave me back my youth in a wonderful way. As long as we had that, we were great. We had no past; the present was great...."

"Unfortunately there was a future."

"Aw, come on. You got away to the city. You had your women and adventures. You got a degree, set up a career. You can't tell me you're sad about all that."

"Then why am I back?"

"You tell me. But first I'll tell you one last thing about the old you and me. When I stopped pretending I had no past, I finally started to understand why I was so willing to burn all my bridges for you. It was rebellion. I swore up and down to myself at the time that it wasn't, that I was just in love. But every time the school board threatened to fire me because of you, I felt great, purified. I had proven that I wasn't going to let other people's notions of what was proper get me a second time."

"I guess that puts me in my place."

She reached and put her hand on his leg.

"You were a wonderful lover too and I did love you very much. But you were also my way of getting back at, I don't know, at myself for wasting so much good time."

"Youth is always wasted, isn't it?"

She rubbed down hard on his thigh.

"Gabriel, you've grown up great. I like you."

"But you don't entirely want me around."

"No. But I'll pay you a high compliment. I can't believe we made love. I can't believe we're having this conversation."

"Ready to find out why I'm here?"

"Sure."

"To ask you to marry me."

She withdrew her hand, held it in mid-air.

"It's okay. You don't have to refuse right away. I've got a few things I'd like to tell you too."

As they passed through the lights of Beaver Creek, gassed up and continued, Gabriel talked about Hank, which Jennifer either knew from Walter already or had heard in rages from the other, younger Gabriel. But he also told her, for the first time, about his mother. His mother had died of cancer in her breasts, he said; she had not gone to a doctor. She had wanted to die. In spite of children, she had wanted to die because her husband had left her without leaving her. Because she knew no other way off that farm, could imagine no other future, she picked death.

Now, Hank was also dying. But he wasn't dying alone. He wasn't dying unloved. And Gabriel didn't know what to do about that; he wasn't sure he really wanted revenge anymore but he did want to somehow stick up for the dignity of the otherwise forgotten. Perhaps by starting something fresh and new ...

As he told the story, the van ran along the blacktop west. His words ran out into thoughts. The van turned north onto gravel. The tires roared. Stones fired off the chassis. And underneath the noise, a single thought formed and harped.

Why is she taking me home?

A precise half-mile before that turning, Jennifer took Winterspeer's road, and a hundred yards before Winterspeer's yardlight, she dipped through the shallow ditch and bumped along a rutted trail that wound around sloughs and dove through buckbrush hollows. Cowflap licked up and whipped in the wheelwells. At the top of a long grade she stopped. Gabriel thought he ought to have known where they were but didn't in the darkness.

She shut down the engine, the lights. A rapid ticking in the block, the only sound between them and silence.

"Where are we?"

"Where we're going to sleep."

She pushed between the seats into the back and worked at clearing and straightening the bed.

"Come."

He crawled in with her, shed his clothes out onto the floor, accepted her rule of silence. He wrapped in round her and slept.

She shook him awake and it felt too soon.

The morning was only grey, the horizon faintly pink.

"Can't we sleep?"

"In a little while. I want us to see the dawn."

They dressed and she gave him an apple to eat and clean his teeth on. He shucked the van door back and they climbed down into the damp bite of morning. On opposite sides of the van they pissed, ridiculous noise, as the blood red dawn stirred among the hills. She came round the front of the van and beckoned.

He followed her down the ridge, knowing now where he was. It was the view of more than half a lifetime slightly altered by perspective: Winterspeer's half-section, near the fence to their own. But Jennifer led him the other way, down the ridgeline south to a rocky portion on its eastern fringe. She disappeared below the jam of rocks and, when he found her, she was sitting on the far side of a small grotto out of which a clear stream trickled.

"Did you know this was here?"

"I guess not."

"I love springs. The idea of something new beginning. I always follow the water up. Come. Sit."

He sat on the near side of the spring, put his arm across the rock that roofed it. She reached so their arms rested comfortably together. They watched the sun rupture the skin of horizon.

"Go ahead," she said.

He was surprised, wondered what; then knew.

"Okay. Will you marry me?"

She turned to him, the full lips smiling. She took his hand and kissed the knuckles.

"No," she said.

Gabriel flopped back, closed his eyes, laughed. She was tugging on his shirtsleeve.

"But know this, Gabriel. You bastard. I honestly couldn't decide that until this minute and it should never have been that hard."

They were both laughing by then and it was alright.

25

His first proposal of marriage rebuffed, the feeling that the future must be sewn up quickly lingered in Gabriel — just as he himself lingered in Jennifer's apartment. Wanting to settle everything, he could settle nothing. Jennifer, for her part, simply allowed him to stay as, he supposed, the last thing she could do for him. Give him time to think, without pressure, and with the comfort of her body in bed next to his.

Time to think became its own kind of pressure when Gabriel could not seem to think at all. In the hours when Jennifer was at school, Gabriel sat in a broad and frozen silence. If he didn't take specific precautions against them, the words "Who if not Jennifer?" would skitter across that silence. The words implied a search, one he had no zest for; just the idea tired him out.

So, he rested. He took to bed in mid-afternoon and waited for four o'clock. When he heard Jennifer clipping down the outside steps, the door slam, the dumping of books onto the kitchen table, the thing inside him loosened off a little, gave him some peace.

On the longest day of the year, the sound was different. What Jennifer did as she entered the basement was the same but the sound was changed; brighter and quicker somehow. When she came into the bedroom, Gabriel saw more to disquiet him: a giddiness, a schoolgirl excitement. She almost said what it was, but then decided on more ceremony. She pulled him out of bed, told him to dress. They were going for a drive.

On the top of Winterspeer's hill, she trotted ahead to the spring. She plunked down on the far side and waited. Gabriel took his place across the water.

She reached her hand out to him. He took it.

"I handed in my resignation today. I'm booked on a flight to Athens second Tuesday in July." Her eyes were on the east horizon, the line indistinct now that the sun had so long abandoned it. "The beauty is, I don't know when or even if I'll be back."

He pressed her hand, withdrew his, and said, "Good. Good for you."

In the airport, Gabriel took pictures. Her tanned, tough arms, sticking out of rolled sleeves, making cup handles to her waist. The bulging backpack clanked when she hefted it for another shot. Everything she wanted was in that pack. To take more would fetter the dive into what she called "perfect blue."

A pair of twenty-year-olds, bent under the weight of their fluorescent orange and blue packs (Canadian flags neatly sewn on the flaps), came up and asked Jennifer for advice on travel to foreign lands. "Great tan," the young fellow said and then looked hurt when Gabriel and Jennifer laughed. It wasn't their fault; she did look like she was coming back, not leaving.

Jennifer insisted on going through the security check early, before a line had a chance to form. A clean, neat parting; for Gabriel, an incision. He apologized for his mournfulness. He held her tight, breathed deep her smell of suntan oil and wind. She talked into his hair about the nice place they had built in their lives to look back on, about futures wonderfully unmapped. Then she held him at arm's length, turned and tossed her shoulder bag on the conveyor. She stepped quickly through the wooden frame.

HANK   And the skies are not cloudy
        All day

Gabriel went back to the basement suite and lived. Mrs. Albert who owned the house and lived upstairs said she had seen everything now. She hadn't approved of the goings on downstairs but "you two were so good together." She left pans of sticky squares on the step outside his door.

After one rent payment, Gabriel's money was gone. He went to work at one of the plants, a labouring job during plant turn-around. The superintendent was disappointed in him for taking the job — an insult to the engineering degree that both of them held — but an engineer at labourer's wages was too good a deal to pass up.

In the evenings of that summer, Gabriel went fishing. He bought a canoe and rowed himself around the plant's cooling water dam. When it got lonely, he phoned Winterspeer. Walter came out but would not fish. He tied bread to a hookless line and dragged it behind the boat — keeping his relationship with nature pure. Walter often heard that Hank had died, only to see him in the truck beside Lyla the next day.

The rumours:
  Hank was in line for the first artificial heart in Canada.
  Hank had nothing wrong with him except that he was a drunk. His time away had been spent in Ponoka, drying out.
  Hank was on his way to the Philippines to have a growth removed from his chest by a bloodless surgeon. "They massage a pore in the skin until it spreads right open. The old Philippino doctor reaches in and rips the things right out. Art Bowley got his cancer out that way and had it in a jar by his bed right to the day he died."

In late August, Gabriel met Lyla on Main Street in Beaver Creek. They went for coffee. Hank was about the same, she said. A local doctor wanted to see him but Hank had forced the sawbones to admit nothing could be done. "Then figure out some other way of getting your million out of Medicare." It was worse still when the priest came. Head bowed, hands folded. "What's ailing you?" Hank asked him. "Somebody die?" When Hank told the priest he was worse than a buzzard, the man fled, pitching signs of the cross over his shoulder. Oh, and by the way, Lyla said, Alice Christoff was back at home. But Joe was still in hiding.

Not long after, Gabriel left Beaver Creek.

    CLIVE: The universe is collapsing. Gabriel, the engine of free enterprise, on POGEY?
    GABRIEL: I didn't say I couldn't get a job. I just don't feel like looking right now.
    CLIVE: The rot engendered by the welfare state; have you ever observed a better example, Phipps?
    PHIPPS: Atlas shrugs.
    GABRIEL: You still queer, Phipps?
    PHIPPS: No, I gave it up. It was worse than the other. I'm asexual now.
    CLIVE: A sexual what? Pervert?
    PHIPPS: You shouldn't act stupid, Clive. You're not smart enough. People will believe you.
    CLIVE: Phipps is just sore because he wrote his Métis poem and the organizers wouldn't let him read it at the Batoche Centennial or whatever it was.
    PHIPPS: They said there wasn't room on the agenda but I know it's because I'm white.
    CLIVE: Wouldn't you know it? Even the Natives have gone nativist.

Lyla's phone call came in the middle of the night. Gabriel was in his shorts; the apartment was cold. After hanging up, he went to the living room, sat and lit a smoke. Beyond the balcony, the city's lights reflected down off a low November sky. Lyla's voice had been ragged, full of tears; saying, you *must come*. I need you *now*. He saw himself shaking hands, fielding condolences, eating little cakes the neighbour women dropped by.

Hank had not tricked the doctors after all, the priests — above all, not the roadblocks on his own blood highway. After one last summer, one last fall, gravity had won, as gravity always does.

"There isn't going to be any funeral."

Lyla and Gabriel sat at the scratched arborite kitchen table, a whisky bottle between them. Above, a naked lightbulb on a dusty two-foot cord: a sixty-watt nose drop, frozen. Lyla was rattled, and drunk. The parts of her face not stained by tears and leaching makeup were blotched red and white. Gabriel had expected something different: that she would possess a frightening calm, give a show of strength that people would talk about, admiringly, for a long time.

"Come on, Lyla, there has to be a funeral. Can't put him in the ground with no show at all."

"Is everybody in this goddamn country a bureaucrat now? I say *no* funeral and *no* burial either, not in their cemetery anyway."

"I guess you'd like to leave him on top."

"He asked to be buried in the hill. And I promised he would be."

"Jesus Christ, what hill?"

"What hill do you think? The same one your grandfather's in. Same way, standing up."

"Lyla, there's a place for him beside my mother in town and that's where he's going. We'll bury him there, horizontal. For once, we're going to do things like normal people do them."

Lyla stood, the backs of her knees slamming the chair into the wall. She reached and grabbed Gabriel by the shirt, shook him back and forth. A button popped and skittered away across the linoleum. He took hold of her wrists.

"You bastard, Gabriel. I knew you'd do this. You're so goddamn proud that your grandfather's up there. But when Hank asks the same, it's stupid."

She twisted her wrists free, raked her fingers back through her tightly braided hair, the strands snapping. "Well, I'll tell you something, smallfry, it's *his* farm. He spent as long here as anyone. It was his dying wish and it's going to happen, if I have to steal the body and dig the hole myself."

"Steal the body."

"You don't see it lying around here, do you? I knew he was dead but I called the ambulance anyway. Next thing he was being zipped into a bag and they were taking him to town. He's in a box there and I've got to steal him back."

Lyla slid down onto her chair. She buried her head in crossed arms on the table. She spoke more but her voice was too low and muffled to hear. The black soak of tears spread out through the pale denim sleeve.

Gabriel and Lyla stood in dark clothes at the back door of McCludden's Funeral Home. They were looking at a pair of deadbolts, a sign that said "This Property Protected by Burglar Alarm," barred windows. The tinsnips in Lyla's hand, the gooseneck bar in Gabriel's, seemed flimsy; like they were about to attack a prison fence with fingernail clippers.

"You'd think," said Lyla, "with all the movies and TV a person sees, we'd be able to figure this right out. Should we cut the power line maybe?"

"And fry ourselves, sure."

"How about a diversion? We could set the old garbage dump on fire. Or, I know! We should get a midget!"

A good part of a bottle of whisky had gone down Lyla in loud swigs in the truck.

"A midget."

"You know, to go through the bars."

"If you know one with a four-inch diameter skull, give him a call."

The power line Lyla wanted to cut gave Gabriel an idea. He led the way round the side to where the line entered the building, pointed his flashlight in the nearest basement window. A narrow utility room: mop in a pail, washer and dryer, a small freezer and, as he'd hoped, a breaker box, its grey corner just visible to the left. He searched the edges of the window for wires, saw none. He asked Lyla to take off her shearling-lined coat and hold it over his hands while he pressed. Even at that the glass broke with enough noise to rouse a neighbour's dog; a hound that bayed.

Gabriel swept the glass from the frame and pushed an arm between the concrete and the first bar. The door of the breaker box was open and he ran his fingers down the rows of switches until he came to the large one across the bottom. He gave it a shove and the orange light on the freezer blinked out.

At the rear door again, they pried on the gooseneck. A screech of screws ripping from wood and the deadbolt housing fell on the ground. A half dozen dogs were howling as they let themselves inside.

They were in a rear porch. Two doors, three counting the now powerless elevator, faced them. Gabriel gave the door closest to him a shove and his flashlight beam pushed through and down a hallway from back to front of the building. They followed the hall to where it opened into a large front room smelling of flowers and scented candles. Chairs were lined up in rows; flowers puffed out of wall sconces. Beside them, a coffin stood on a carpeted dais with flowers round the base.

"Hope it's him."

"Who else?"

"Somebody at the old folks' home died."

"Don't you recognize the box?"

"Never seen it. Just told the undertaker to put him in the cheapest he had."

"Great."

"Does it look cheap?"

"I've never priced them."

"Aw shit, let's stop being such chickenshits and look."

They moved to the short end of the two-piece lid. Gabriel opened it, a soft hydraulic sigh. He shone the light in and Lyla peeked over his shoulder.

"Shit."

"Recognize the guy?"

"No."

"Guess it makes sense. I didn't order all these flowers or ask for prayers."

"Must be in the basement then. Most of the rest of this floor has to be garage."

Back in the porch, the second door opened onto stairs. "This is creepier than hell, in case you haven't noticed," said Lyla, going down.

A sign at the bottom said "Preparation Room." The rubber-stripped door opened like a freezer. A smell lept up their nostrils as it did. Not a bad smell really; if it had come from any other place, it would have seemed harmless. But perfumes masking chemicals brought visions of men in gory coveralls brutalizing the dead.

The flashlight swept another large room. Two empty tables with tight stretched plastic covers. A third platform on wheels held a coffin identical to the one upstairs. Beside the empty table farthest from the coffin, a pump gizmo was attached to a large jar of moon-coloured fluid. They had to admit that the undertaker ran a clean shop. None of the black blood Gabriel thought the place might be clotted with; no plastic garbage bags, slack-weighted.

"Jesus, look at this."

Lyla was running her flashlight along the lines of carefully hand-stencilled signs tacked up on the rear wall.

When conducting a home removal,

DO NOT yank on the straps
OR operate the stretcher cover zipper
in a rapid way,
OR swing the deceased.
Such actions often upset the bereaved.

Lift with the legs.
Keep the back in an
upright position.

DO NOT casket the deceased
until fully dressed and cosmeticized.

"Cosmeticized! What the hell is that?"
"Probably not as bad as it sounds. Come on, let's get this thing moving."
"The rate people are dying around here, we better check."
She opened the lid. Gabriel waited but she didn't say anything. From where he was watching, the light gave the impression of glowing up out of the box: the scene in a horror movie just before the person looking in is grabbed or ignites and dematerializes, leaving a pair of smoking rubber boots. He joined her to see what was wrong.
"Ah, Hank," she sighed. "It is you, sort of."
The face in the box was Hank, sort of. A bloodless mask more like Madame Tussaud's than life. The undertaker had probably never seen Hank alive and had given him a look of quiet meditation he'd never had. Gabriel reached past Lyla's shoulder and closed the lid.
Getting Hank up the stairs was not easy. Bumping a step at a time, they eventually made it. Gabriel half expected to find the police, the fire department and half the town waiting for them, but the entry and the parking lot were empty. The dogs were quiet, past caring. Lyla got the truck and backed it in. They shot the casket over the tailgate and tied a grain tarp flat across the rim of the truck box so no shape would show. They departed laughing: a successful criminal debut.

29

At the farm, they left the truck in the yard. The half-frozen November ground and a load in back would have meant distinct tracks up the hill for the cops to follow. So they carried the box.

A bit of moon glimpsed out of clouds that were scudding fast. Down on the ground, it was still. Just enough light to define the buckbrush and willow thickets, the alleys of dead grass. Carrying the coffin was slow work that made the arms wooden before much of the hill was climbed. Finally, the coffin slammed to the ground as if of its own accord. Gabriel went back for a horse.

He caught and saddled Hank's palomino, with some vague sense that this horse had to be the one to do the job. The gelding threw its head, snorted, acted berserk. When it heard the fence posts knocking in the lariat noose, it shied and almost fell to its knees; the feel of the posts coming up behind scared him even more and he surged. Gabriel hauled on the reins, sawed the bit in the hard mouth. But every whisper of wind in a willow bunch, every rattle of a rabbit moving deeper into brush, made the bastard plunge and shy.

Through this fight, Gabriel aimed for a dense pocket of black on the hill above them. When they got close and Lyla stood up, splitting that dark spot suddenly in two, the gelding reared its neck into Gabriel's face. He saw bright lights, then a jump forward unsnapped his thighs from the saddle bulges. The hard ground came up through the darkness and hit him hard enough to knock the air out. To her credit, Lyla managed to lay hold of the reins when they flew out of Gabriel's hand.

It was quite a while before he had sufficient air to say, "I always hated that sonofabitching horse."

"Ssh, now, babe," Lyla said, and not to Gabriel, for whom she seemed to have no sympathy. "I'll ride him. He probably knows me better. He certainly likes me better."

"My guest."

The next step was for Gabriel to thread the lariat through the coffin handles and for Lyla to tie the rope off on the horn. They moved again. Gabriel lifted the coffin onto one fencepost and, as Lyla eased the horse ahead and the coffin rolled over this post, Gabriel ran ahead and set another between the horse's heels and the coffin's prow. If he was fast enough, collecting the rear post when it rolled free and running ahead to reset it at the front, they could keep moving fairly steadily. While he worked, Lyla lay forward along the horse's neck, rubbing the rigid flesh and talking gently.

At last: the pines. The illumined rock spine of the hill above them shone like the plated backbone of a dinosaur whenever the flowing cloud opened a pocket for the moon. Lyla went to tether the jittery, sweat-soaked gelding well away from the box. Gabriel flopped in the lee of the casket, barely able to feel amongst the other discomforts the cold damp soaking up into his pants. He was practically asleep by the time Lyla dropped beside him. She pulled the whisky bottle from the warm envelope of breasts and sheepskin. The first one she'd flung off into the ditch between Beaver Creek and the farm, but this one was full. The clouds grew in masses out of the mountains, moved between the ragged shoulders of the trees. The wind had picked up a little, enough to yaw the trunks and rattle the branches. The whisky burned down. The bit of contact their shoulders made along the slick surface of wood seemed like conversation enough; that and the movement of the sloshing bottle back and forth. Later, Lyla did talk, in a low voice that blurred or got lost in the wind. She talked about Hank and her, stuff you wouldn't expect to know about your father. They'd never stopped making love, she said, even when he was having trouble getting from the kitchen to the bedroom under his own steam. They tried and once in awhile succeeded. "If I die on top of you, don't feel guilty," he said. "That's exactly how I want it to be." He had almost convinced her it would happen that way, though his rages were a better bet to bring on the end. Oh yes, he'd kept that up too. Not about Gabriel or Joe, though; he'd settled that somehow in his mind. What came in for most of the abuse was God. The burning sewer was what he called hell. Gyp your neighbour or sleep with his wife and you're for it. God's rules. The closer he came to the end the more he seemed to need to ridicule the idea of there being anything more.

Lyla confessed to Gabriel that she did believe in some form of God and, though she'd never told Hank, she prayed for him quite often. Asked God to be reasonable. If Hank had believed, he wouldn't have said all those things. Not believing seemed the most forgivable thing.

But she didn't really want to talk about his anger. It was the quiet in him she preferred to speak of now. He liked to sleep with his head on the softest part of her belly. Her hands in his hair, one of his hands cupped round her thigh. He liked to be held onto, to hold on. "He was very warm for a skinny man," she said.

When the hissing in his head outdistanced the wind, Gabriel realized he was drunk. He said so and Lyla answered, "Good. Best for both of us to be blind tonight."

By then, Lyla had talked herself out. Gabriel started some ramblings of his own. He talked about Jennifer and how, in the end, she'd wanted what she did not know more than she wanted him. She was probably right but it seemed hopeless most of the time now that she was gone.

Gabriel wanted a woman, the right one, but looking.... Shit, just the thought of looking....

He even told Lyla about the mythical woman who'd seemed so close to his touch, swirling a veil made of northern lights. That was the night after the night they'd met, when he'd gone floundering in the snow to Winterspeer's to avoid her. That woman of lights seemed more real than the lady who was supposed to be waiting for him in his future.

Lyla turned so more of her body rested against his. Her forehead still on the hard surface of the box. Hank's head was just a few inches away, she said. That was death for you. It might always feel like that. Hank just a little ways away but across something solid and invisible that you couldn't cross without dying.

When she kissed him, Gabriel wasn't offended, nor even surprised. He wanted her to. Liked the whisky taste that fused across their tongues. He wanted to give her something. Had nothing else. She reached inside his jacket, moved her hands up and down his ribs. Then she sat back and took off her coat. She laid it fleece up on the ground.

Gabriel studied her face in the low light for a minute, then took his own coat off. He placed it end to end with hers and reached for her. She kissed him one more time, deep and long, and then she withdrew. She picked her coat back up and brushed off the pine needles.

"What's wrong?"

"Nothing," she said. "I'm sorry. I just had to see if you would."

"I don't get it."

"You're a good man, Gabriel. Willing to go a long way to console a woman twice your age, and that's good. Don't be too hostile if I say it's the best thing you've got in common with your old man."

The arrival of the RCMP the next morning was an event perceived or recorded by no one. The two constables stepped out of the car, one flexing the yellow stripe in his pants while the other straightened his hat brim. They were formal even for Mounties and someone accustomed to the species might have noted in their behaviour the symptoms of reluctance.

Standing in the angle of their open car doors, they searched the yard for someone to make their statement to. The doors of the outbuildings were closed and latched. The only signs of humanity were two trucks parked with their grills pointing to the house, and a horse tethered in the fenceless yard ripping up grass. Saddle and blanket were dumped in a pile a few yards away. Taking the initiative, the driver strode to the house door and knocked. The old screen twanged like a sprung banjo. He took off his hat, slid it under the arm he kept stiff to one side, wiped a hand across his hair. He had to knock a few more times before a tall woman in a terry cloth housecoat opened the inside door.

A sad picture. Her hair in braids but the hair half out of them, looking even more messy for the attempt at order. Bosom framed by the faded cloth overlap. Breasts nippling in the morning air. Her eyes were bloodshot and the smell of whisky sieved out the screen. She was in mourning, the constable reminded himself, and would be more so with this news.

The constable showed his identification through the screen.

"Constable Wark. R.C.M.P. Beaver Creek detachment. Are you Mrs. Lyla Pryde?"

"Mizzz Lyla Pryde."

"You are the person listed as the one to call regarding the funeral arrangements of Mr. Hank Spikes?"

"That's right."

"Are you Mr. Spikes' wife?"

"I was his lover."

The constable stiffened and blinked.

"I have some bad news."

"Can't be as bad as the news around here generally."

"I'm sorry, maybe you've already heard then. . . ."

"If you're here to tell me Hank's dead, you're a little slow on the draw."

"Actually no. The news is that his body's been stolen from the undertaker's and, so far, we haven't. . . ."

"Except for you don't look like you ever told a joke, I'd say you must be joking."

"I'm afraid it's true."

"Jesus, what next!"

"I'm sure I don't know. There'll be an investigation of course."

"Good of you. Meanwhile I've got a funeral scheduled and no one to bury."

"I really can't help you there."

Lyla Pryde laughed and Constable Wark wasn't sure what he'd said that was funny.

Back in the car, Constable Wark's partner reminded him that the woman was not technically next-of-kin. There were sons, a pair of them, somewhere. On the verge of going back in to inquire about these sons, the driver's seat Mountie got the brainwave of radioing in the license plate numbers of the trucks in the yard. The computer check revealed that Gabriel of the same last name as the deceased, aged twenty-five, was the registered owner of the half-ton. That was good enough. They left the yard, planning how to investigate the break-in at the funeral home and the theft of what was remaining of Mr. Hank Spikes.

The black wall phone was the focus of much activity that day. Many messages went out and, if the phone was in its cradle for more than a couple of minutes, it rang. Horrified townspeople and neighbours called one after another, anxious to convey the news. They told it first as if it were verified gospel but, as soon as they found out Gabriel and Lyla knew, they asked, "Is it really true then?" In a place that had known its share of the bizarre and the grisly, this was a new one.

The telephone line being a party line, the outgoing calls had to be coded. When Gabriel picked up the phone, he could usually hear sounds from someone else's house — faint radio or the muffled cry of a baby. While he spoke, these sounds were joined by others until there was an orchestra of breathing, dog barking, cough-stifling between himself and whomever he was calling.

Always alert to conspiracy, Clive caught Gabriel's tone immediately. "I'll be down as fast as Phipps can drive." Lucky too that Clive was so perceptive, because Phipps himself, when called, missed the point by miles. He was sorry that Gabriel's father had died but he really couldn't consider coming down right now. He was in the midst of another draft of his epic poem about Batoche. He had decided that, even though he'd been denied the chance to read it at the official commemoration, he would go to Batoche before the year's end and read it in the graveyard. "It is a work of the spirit and I'll read it to those most likely to appreciate it: the spirits of the dead of Batoche."

Grazing close to the truth, Gabriel argued that Phipps had all the more reason to come down to the farm then. "Instead of dreaming about history, this is your big chance to make some." Ever suspicious, Phipps asked how. Talk to Clive, Gabriel said and hung up.

Winterspeer asked what time he should come over the next day before Gabriel had a chance to speak at all. Walter was on the same party line and a compulsive rubberneck.

To drag scent across the trail, Lyla phoned the *Beaver Creek Bugle* and dictated a distressed letter to appear in the following week's edition. It ended with a plea that anyone with the slightest clue to the whereabouts of Hank's body should please send word to the box number listed below. The editor of the *Bugle*, astounded at his luck, said he would of course run the letter, and free of charge, in this week's paper even though the deadline was technically past.

That left only one call to make. Gabriel phoned the Christoff place down the road, and got Alice's father on the line. "Is this that goddamn Joe?!"

On the second try, it was Mr. Christoff again:

"You damn fool, you think I'd let my daughter marry some creep whose father goes around having his corpse stolen?!"

Gabriel persevered and eventually got Alice. He spoke quickly. If she knew where Joe could be found would she please tell him to come home.

"Joe should be here to help."

That was a lame one. Help with what? But she said she'd try.

Lyla knew a thing or two about dynamite. You needed a government permit to buy it and.... Say no more, said Gabriel. He drove up the Crowsnest Pass that morning, kept going until the air stank of coke furnaces and the houses and people were stained by soot. He found a miner's bar in the shadow of the slag heaps and offered to buy beer for the only other patron, a man too young to be so gnarled and to have so much coal soot darkening his creases and pores.

Drinking Gabriel's beer, the man wanted to know what election it was. When Gabriel said he needed dynamite, the man's expression changed; suspicion left him. Gabriel told the miner he was a farmer with stumps to blow. He didn't feel like going through all the government rigamarole. But the subterfuge was barely necessary. "Need dynamite" was all the man needed to hear and all he listened to.

31

When the first vehicle rolled in, it was too late to wonder how it was all going to look to the neighbours. If the code had fooled the rubbernecks, they were safe; if not, they were doomed. Winterspeer was the first: with whisky, beer and, under a tarp in the back of his truck, digging tools. This chipped away at Gabriel's confidence for he had said nothing in their phone conversation about digging. But Winterspeer insisted they were safe. He had rubbered every single outgoing call and had been more than a little impressed by Gabriel's slight of word. Only someone like himself with extensive prior knowledge could have possibly figured out that digging was implied. They began to drink.

Phipps and Clive pulled in a few hours later. They found Gabriel with Lyla and Winterspeer in the kitchen, slightly drunk. The two from the city had beer too, but nothing else, not even gloves. Clive had sensed urgency, conspiracy and possibly adventure, but he had no idea really why they were there. Told by Gabriel, both were pleased, even though neither had much track record in the matter of digging. Clive had never turned over soil for any purpose not even a garden. Phipps had dug only once, a tunnel under the back fence of his parents' yard; he'd been caught before he could escape.

Phipps had worn an owly expression when first he came in the door — the interruption of his poem. That mood began to change as he realized the epic dimensions of the experience he'd left it for. White man to join Métis in the standing burial ground. Symbolic implications of the acceptance of the settler's sin? Or, just the opposite: an invasion of sanctuary, the final intrusion of white upon Métis, even unto the ground their dead inhabited? Large themes at any rate, to be mulled over and seen through to their various ends.

For Clive, it was the criminal aspect that appealed: a federal government employee participating in a conspiracy to rob government ground of a Canadian corpse. If caught, his career would be wrecked and that terrified him. Like most politicians, though, complete or in the bud, Clive liked to flirt close to the flame.

The newcomers got into the beer quickly; or, if the truth be told, got into it more deeply. Among the cases they trundled from the car was one which had been deeply pillaged en route.

What were they waiting for? The question arose as the room began to darken. Two things, said Gabriel: night, and his brother Joe. They had to wait for night, that was imperative; but, after the darkness had arrived, they would not wait any longer for Joe. He had too much potential for not showing up at all.

But, with the lights on in the house and Gabriel going over the first stage of his plan, a motorcycle did thunder into the yard. Joe burst into the kitchen and showed every sign of wanting to burst back out again. He looked at Walter, Lyla, at the peculiar city people (extraterrestrials, to his eyes) and he performed a magic trick; he disappeared into himself.

Gabriel grabbed his brother's arm and jerked him down into a chair. He introduced him around quickly and went on with the plan.

Joe didn't say anything while Gabriel spoke. He did begin to fidget and to scratch. He scratched everywhere but his balls, but you could tell he wanted to scratch those too. The minute the group was outside, Joe took hold of Gabriel's coat sleeve and dragged him round the corner of the house.

"I ain't going to do it."

"Why not?"

"It's stupid, that's fuckin' why. I'm in enough shit as it is."

He sucked himself in and wiggled the snuff can out of the tight rear squeeze of his jeans. He pinched a wad into his lip. "Alice's knocked up," he said. "If Christoff gets wind of this too, he'll go apeshit."

Gabriel understood then that Joe was in the process of trading one boss for another.

"He won't do anything because he won't know."

"You can't tell me what to do."

"Listen, you dumb asshole, the Old Man left the farm to me and you."

As Gabriel thought it might, the news drenched Joe in immediate happiness. He didn't have the wit or stagecraft to hide it.

"As far as I'm concerned, that means he left it to you. What he wanted back was to be buried up there. By rights you oughta be digging the hole yourself."

Troops deployed. Lyla aboard Gallant, dragging tools by lariat. The others carried mostly bottles, in two parties led by Joe and Gabriel. Three well separate routes, so as not to create a path investigators of these doings could easily follow.

Another rule: no flashlights during the climb.

Cloud smothered moon, wind absent. Gabriel could hear everything. The clicking of the horse's fetlocks to his right, the jangle of dragging tools. Farther away in that direction, bottle music. The novices tripping and falling, cursing and apologizing.

Lyla and Gallant were invisible in the larger shadow of pines, waiting as the two foot parties converged. Night blind, Phipps walked directly into the horse's ass. Was lucky not to be kicked to death. Leaping away, he toppled over the coffin, smashing a beer bottle to glass and froth between his chest and the wood.

"Okay, we'll leave one lantern on," said Gabriel.

Lyla picked the spot; Gabriel accepted the choice. He drove a crowbar in to mark it. Then he outlined the second stage of his plan.

Three teams of two. One crowbar and one shovel working at a time. Everybody should work as fast as possible, and, as soon as one team began to tire, it was to get the hell out of the hole and make way for the next.

The hole did not go down quickly. At this altitude, at this point in a cold November, the frost was already down. The ground chipped out like hoof trimmings. Phipps and Winterspeer made up one team, laureates composing verse as they flailed away. Phipps versified on themes of resistance and penetration; the indifferent earth split (they hoped) to contain the flesh, bones and box of this white man. Did his Métis predecessor, already in the earth's tight embrace, and by genetics more comfortable there, did he smile at their exertions, did he exert supernatural influence against their success?

For Winterspeer, more earthly lines of reasoning suggested themselves:

> The spring is broken
> The Jack in this box
> Will pop up no more.

And a lot of other verses with the refrain:

> Oh, oh, this fucking ground,
> This fucking, unforgiving ground,
> Oh, this fucking ground
> Is hard.

The team of Joe and Clive were more inclined to get on with the job. More "goal-oriented" was Clive's way of putting it. Joe drove the bar into the flinty earth with demented gusto. Pausing and, if Clive didn't instantly scoop the shards from the shallow bowl, whipping the shovel from his hands and doing it himself.

Clive's mind worked swiftly too, but in the direction of laboursaving innovations. Was it necessary, really, to bury the whole box? The corpse alone would be considerably shorter. "Mind your own business," said Lyla.

Lyla and Gabriel, in their turn, ripped through the bottom of the frost and levity took the group as full shovels of rock and clay lowered the hole. The Winterspeer-Phipps team set down bottles, leapt into the hole with good team spirit — and promptly thunked the crowbar into a shelf of stone.

The hole was not two feet deep. Gabriel recognized the stone as the same limestone sill he and Joe had picked and shovelled at as boys to bury Baptiste. It was even shallower here as the sill was surfacing from north to south. Gabriel had hoped it would not present itself, that it would have faulted away somehow, but now that it was here he did have a plan for it. He let the teams beat away at the stone for awhile, making little impression, listening to a litany of increasing invention from Clive as he more thoroughly exercised his imagination on ways to make this labour cease. Not only could Hank be buried boxless, but wouldn't the old fighter be just as happy — more comfortable, in fact — sitting to take in the view? For that matter, had anyone considered the option of cremation? The hole, while not deep, was deep enough to accommodate a few well spread fistfuls of ash.

"We're buryin' him whole," said Lyla, "and that's that."

Gabriel chose this moment to issue fresh instructions.

Everyone should now concentrate on hollowing out one crowbar-sized hole in the middle to a depth of about ten inches. Joe snapped a look at his brother.

When the smaller hole was down, Gabriel produced a stick of dynamite from his coveralls and, in the way of a magician, showed it around. "Gabriel, you prick!" Clive cried, showing him a bulb of blister like a pink slug on his thumb. Gabriel waited in silence for the mutterings to cease then gave details of what he called *Stage 2-A*.

Everyone but Joe and Gabriel were to return to the farmhouse. In the yard, they would find a partly full gas can. Threaded from its nozzle was a fuse which extended back to the house. At the stroke of midnight, one hour from now, that fuse was to be lit, thus blowing up the gas can and starting a fire. They would be ready, with water and the extinguisher from Gabriel's truck, to put it out.

Meanwhile, also exactly on the stroke of midnight, Gabriel would be lighting a fuse the identical length up on the hill. The explosion of dynamite in Hank's hole would in this way be synchronized to the explosion of the gas can.

Gabriel held up the lantern and surveyed the faces. Joe: horrified. Phipps and Clive: mystified. Winterspeer: pie-eyed. Lyla: satisfied — in that the plan was a good part hers. She tapped her watch face and Winterspeer called out the time on his so all could synchronize time pieces.

Only Joe had anything to say.

"This bloody thing's out of control."
Gabriel ignored him and completed the instructions.
After they had put out the gas can fire, they were to wait at the house for an hour and a half before coming back up. If police, fire department or neighbours presented themselves, they were to act drunk (no problem there) and explain that they had been using gasoline to burn garbage earlier in the day. They'd put the fire out, or so they thought, but evidently it had gotten away in the grass, reaching and exploding the gas can.

The explosions had about them a festive quality. Like Chinese New Year or Greek Easter. The ground shook under Gabriel and Joe, lying behind their respective trees. Rocks and clumps of root rained down on their legs. The plume of fire in the yard missed simultaneity by mere seconds. Looking down, Gabriel could see tiny figures in the fire glow, throwing buckets of water, spraying with the extinguisher. It was soon out. Joe and Gabriel entered their crump hole and began digging.

An hour or so later, a vehicle did pass under them into the yard, a car. It stayed about a quarter hour. There was no one else and, when the others returned to the hill top, they said that the visitors were Mounties, the same two who had been out the other day. They had been alerted by a neighbour to the north who described a fearful explosion and a flash like lightening behind the hill.

The Mounties had accepted the gas can explanation. They shook their heads knowingly, human folly being their business. The older of the two recounted how often he had known one tragedy to follow another. Grief made people careless, as if they courted these disasters. Phipps had become interested. Among the Natives of antiquity, he told the Mounties, it was common for a mourner to cut his flesh, rip his hair out, wear ragged clothing. Did the Mountie think there was any connection, a universal theme, perhaps? They were gone pretty quick after that. Walter phoned Sheila in case she too had been frightened by the blast, but he woke her out of a deep sleep and got an earful of unpleasantness for his trouble.

The hole was down five feet in good going by then. Gabriel had one more stick of dynamite but no plan for explaining the explosion if it were needed. This added a certain tension to the dig, a relief springing each time the bar fell and was not stopped.

Hank had been five foot eight. The box was seven foot, one size fitting all in this economy class. Just shy of seven feet, the bar hit stone. Dull thunking as the bar searched and found no edge.

Stymied so close to the goal, the group fell to cursing and scuffing the ground.

"Wouldn't you fucking well know it?" cried Phipps. He was now so engrossed in this task that his own poem was fading considerably. He felt whole stanzas break off and go whirling, oblivion bound. Truth was, his epic was beginning to feel paltry. After the others had gone to the coffin to sit and drink, Phipps stayed in the hole whacking sparks off the rock with his bar. Crying for dynamite.

With the last stick in his pocket, pressing right against his thigh, Gabriel had long ago decided not to use it. Another blast and the neighbours would have the police, the fire department, the Bow Crow Forest Reserve wardens and half the town of Beaver Creek breathing down their necks.

"Nope," he said, "if we can't go down, we'll go up." "What the goddamn hell now?" Joe wanted to know.

From a rough mental calculation, Gabriel had come up with the figure forty-five cubic feet. When the coffin went in and the hole was filled and well tamped, forty-five cubic feet of dirt should remain. From this a mound could be created. The largest plate of limestone blown off the sill could be left cropping out of the mound as a kind of rain shield and grave marker. Almost everyone applauded this idea and declared it an amazing early redemption of Gabriel's engineering degree. Joe had other thoughts.

"The professor forgot to mention that forty of them forty-five are blown from hell to breakfast."

The time had come to lower Hank in. Lyla got a little emotional. She spoke to the box, kissed it, even kicked it. The pallbearers raised it by its handles and slid it over the lip of the hole. It stood there on end. The time for prayers had come and there weren't any. Even Phipps was dry of words. They all looked to Lyla and she looked back with a certain hostility.

"Just get the damn thing covered up," she said.

They put the capstone in place just as the rose of dawn opened over the hill's rock spine. They were back in the farmhouse, tools and bottles stowed, when the first rays of sun hit the windows.

Winterspeer left first, saddled and ridden by a hard-spurring hangover. Joe went about the same time, trying to be elusive, but confessing when pressed that he would be back. He had to retrieve his gear from a motel room up the Pass. Phipps and Clive waited a day, Clive being unfit to travel at first. He suggested that he might be the next in need of burial. Grinning on his green face, he suggested too that it would be a cracking good mystery plot. A group assembles to illegally bury a corpse. Waking the morning after they've done the deed, they find that one of their number has been killed. All must stay on a day to bury this unfortunate and, come morning, holy Hercule, there's a third. And, let me guess, said Phipps, the last one left standing is stuck with the task of burying himself.

Phipps was not upset with Clive for keeping him; in fact, Phipps was in no hurry to leave at all. He was so delighted with what he'd helped to do that he went up again in the morning to look at their handiwork. He spent a long time and, when he came down, he had the look of a prophet. There are certain places in the world, he proclaimed, that are places of truth. People are powerfully drawn to them; they build pyramids and stone circles on them and later generations become confused; they think they are going there to look at the pyramid or the stone circle when in fact they are obeying the original force. The burial ground above was such a place.

As Clive and Phipps drove out along the driveway the next day, they passed Joe coming in.

That night, Gabriel had to sleep on the couch outside Lyla's room. Joe had moved right back onto his mattress upstairs without a thought that he was displacing Gabriel in the process. Gabriel could have unearthed his own mattress but was disgusted by the idea — or ideas. It wasn't just the thought of grubbing down through the filthy stratigraphy and brushing mouse dirt away before he could sleep; it was also the memory of nights spent with no walls between himself and Joe's feet.

Hours after everyone had gone to bed, Lyla said Gabriel's name softly, and he answered. She asked him to come in and they sat together on the bed, Lyla propped in pillows under the covers and Gabriel in his blue jeans on top. She had the window up and the air squeezing through had the ice lick of deep winter in it. After some time of just sitting, Lyla said, "Time to hit the road."

"You kicking me out again?"

She reached and covered his hand, ran a scratchy thumb over his knuckles.

"Me, stupid, I'm kicking me out. I overheard Joe talking to his Alice. I gather she's knocked up. Wedding plans."

"You're supposed to be looked after, you know."

"I don't need looking after just yet. When I do I won't be looking to Joe."

"What will you do?"

"I don't know. Don't much care either. I got kids all over the map. Guess I might visit some of them. There's a couple of new grandchildren I haven't seen yet. What about you?"

"I don't know either."

"That's good. I think that's good."

Gabriel wished in the following silence that a coyote would howl or that frogs were still chorussing in a slough somewhere. But nature had gone in on itself for the winter.

"I guess we could both head out in the morning. I'll give you a ride to Calgary if you want. Except for your horse. I can't do anything for you there."

"Not my horse." She laughed. "It's Joe's but he wouldn't let Joe ride him. Joe was ready to shoot the poor devil and I guess, if he still wants to, the horse is his to do with."

"Gallant?"

"I did name him. I don't think he had one before." Lyla sat up out of her pillows. She grinned and it tore up all the furrows time had put in her face. She looked young and about to do mischief. "What say we get the hell out of here now?"

Gabriel crept upstairs. By the bit of moonlight through the broken window, Joe was a dark shape on the mattress, covered by an opened-out sleeping bag. Gabriel could only tell the head end from the foot by the smothered rumble of snoring. A good way to remember Joe, actually, as something dark and shapeless that stank and snored.

And that was it: the planetary system put to rest. The old sun had burned up; there was no new sun. The light in future would be shed from down the road.

Lyla was clearing her gear out of the bathroom when Gabriel came downstairs. He crossed the hooked rug to her room. Quickly, he dug in the drawer, down through the old love letters. He pulled the folder off the newspaper-covered bottom and was sliding it inside his coat when a sound made him turn. Lyla stood in the doorway.

"You don't have to look like that," she said. "It's yours."

The note scotch-taped to the refrigerator door read:

It's your farm, Joe.
Except for the west hill.
Plow that up and I'll come back
and kick your ass.
        G.

A mile or so from Beaver Creek, Lyla changed her mind. She asked Gabriel to take her into town and drop her at the bus depot. Parked there in the grey pre-dawn, she shook his hand so hard it hurt. She said, "You'll find your woman, honey. She's looking for you too, you know." She was halfway out when she leaned back to kiss him.

Gabriel glanced once in his rearview as he drove away. Tall figure leaning against a steel signpost. Hat pulled down, chin sunk in the fleece lining of her coat. At the far end of Main Street, a Greyhound was turning in as Gabriel turned out. Above the driver's head, the letters spelled Vancouver.

Thirty miles down the road, Gabriel stopped at a service station circled by trucks. He ordered bacon, eggs, toast and coffee from a tired young waitress who looked like she'd been cramming late nights too hard against early mornings. A country and western radio station banged a tune out of corner speakers, too loud and honky-tonk for this hour as far as Gabriel was concerned. He was the only one who seemed to notice.

A few truckers lowered cups of coffee into themselves and it looked like work: part of the job just like the night they'd just spent driving or sleeping behind the seat. Out the window, their diesels were barking reveille. In one of the booths, a group of farmers complained, something about another federal government budget that had all but ignored them.

When the waitress brought his breakfast, Gabriel tried a joke. She said, "Huh?" He said, "Nothing." She walked away. Now was not the time. Later maybe, when the egg-stained uniform went on a hook and she'd made herself up again to party; then she might listen. The eggs were transparent jelly; the toast looked buttered with a shovel; a plateful of slipperiness that shot down him in no time.

On the way out, Gabriel saw a pay phone and stopped. He knew in that moment how it must end. He found the number in what was left of the yellow pages. He dialed and poured in change. To the man who answered, Gabriel explained quickly where the grave was. Beaver Creek Municipal Cemetary, Catholic section; Gabriel thought it was third row from the west, maybe fourth stone in from the north end. With the name to go by, it was no problem, the man said; the people in charge kept a map.

Gabriel explained the rest and the man said it wasn't the kind of thing they did, taking an order over the phone like that. Gabriel pressed, offered his charge card numbers, the names and dates he wanted carved.

Say, said the man, I know that name. That's the guy whose body was stolen, isn't it? Did they find him, then? No, Gabriel said, but I still want the engraving done. The man became apologetic then; he said it was a sign of how the whole country was going to hell. Under the circumstances, he was going to see what he could do, which was as good as saying he'd do it. He took all the information again, and arrived at what Gabriel would like to see inscribed in addition to names and dates.

"What do you usually put?"

There's no usual about it, the man said; he'd carved just about everything you could think of. Was it the husband of the person already buried there, he wanted to know? In that case, "Beloved Husband" was about as close to a standard as there was.

"Are you still there?"

"I'm still here. Okay, put that."

At the highway, Gabriel waited for the traffic of semis and cattle liners to clear. He looked west into the low cloud, the first flakes starting to squeeze out. On a clear day, he could have seen the mountains from here, the mountain behind the two hills, Baptiste's and Gabriel's. But a curtain of grey had fallen between. It didn't matter, he told himself, and knew it was true. The important thing was knowing it was there. He turned north and picked up speed over the ice-fringed Old Man River.

More Fiction from NeWest Press

HEALING SONG by Margaret Clarke $8.95 paperback

This novel is about the healing power of friendship; about the bond between wife and husband, mother and child, women and women; about the fragility of the human being and the importance of taking the time to nurture others — and oneself.

A NEW-FOUND ECSTASY by Ed Kleiman $8.95 paperback

This collection of stories are all concerned with love and marriage: in some of them the romantic quest for a grail ends happily; in others, it ends with a descent into darkness.

HOUSEBROKEN by Leona Gom $8.95 paperback

"A well written and relentless exploration of processes of love and friendship."
   — *Canadian Book Review Annual*

THE MEASURE OF MIRANDA by Sarah Murphy $8.95 paperback

"Sarah Murphy's first novel . . . pushes us past the limits of social and ethnic identity and has us searching, along with the protagonist, for some glimmer of a universal humanity."
   — *Quill and Quire*, March 1988

PROPERTY OF
NORTHERN LIGHTS
LIBRARY SYSTEM ON
PERMANENT LOAN TO:
MANNVILLE MUNICIPAL LIBRARY